Sea Tales of Ireland

Sea Tales of Ireland for Children

Chosen by Joan Ryan and Gordon Snell

GLENDALE PRESS

First published in Ireland by
THE GLENDALE PRESS
18 Sharavogue
Glenageary Road Upper
Dun Laoghaire
Co. Dublin, Ireland.

ISBN 0 907606 10 5

Cover and Book Design by Q
Typeset by Print Prep (Ireland) Ltd., Dublin
Printed by Mount Salus Press, Dublin

Contents

Acknowledgements

The editors and publishers gratefully acknowledge the kind permission of C.J. Fallon and Co. Ltd to reprint *Cliona's Wave* by Sinéad de Valera. *Country Under Wave* by Alice Furlong was reproduced from *Tales of Fairy Folks, Queens and Heroes,* published by Browne and Nolan Ltd., 1907.

Grateful acknowledgement is also given to the following Sources for illustrative material: *Pictures from Punch* 1891; *Instant Archive Art*, The Graphic Communications Centre Ltd., Kent; and *1800 Woodcuts* by Thomas Bewick and his School, edited by B. Cirker, Dover Publications, New York.

In the event of any copyright holder being overlooked the publishers will be only too pleased to come to an arrangement at the first available opportunity.

Introduction

For Ireland's story-tellers, the sea has been a rich source of tales. Many of the stories that were remembered and told by one generation after another, describe adventures on the waves — and under the waves as well. For the sea has always been mysterious and challenging, and it's no wonder that people have been fascinated by the underwater world.

Some of the stories in this book are about the creatures that live in that world: not just fishes and seals, but beings like the jovial old merman who entertains a fisherman in his ocean cave; or the mermaid who becomes a human wife, but yearns to go back to the sea. Then there are tales of sea maidens and water witches with magic powers, and creatures who try to lure humans to a watery doom. There are tales of amazing deeds and perilous journeys, of battles with giants and enormous fishes, of revenge and treachery, boasting and bravado.

There are tales that would make you long to seek out that wondrous ocean world, and others that would make you afraid to go anywhere near the water.

Some of these stories were first written down by collectors of folk-tales like Crofton Croker and Jeremiah Curtin. Some were first published in magazines more than a century ago, and others are by more modern authors such as Sinéad de Valera and Seamus MacManus. But all of them have that sense of excitement about the strange world of the ocean waves.

Like the stories in our first collection, *Land of Tales*, these are good stories for reading aloud as well as reading to yourself, and they show again the great wealth of imagination and delight to be found in Ireland's story-telling tradition.

Joan Ryan and Gordon Snell

FOR LEONARD AND MAEVE
WITH MUCH LOVE

The Soul Cages

by THOMAS CROFTON CROKER

Jack Dogherty lived on the coast of the County Clare. Jack was a fisherman, as his father and grandfather before him had been. Like them, too, he lived all alone (but for the wife), and just in the same spot. People used to wonder why the Dogherty family were so fond of that wild situation, so far away from all human kind, and in the midst of huge shattered rocks, with nothing but the wide ocean to look upon. But they had their own good reasons for it.

The place was just the only spot on that part of the coast where anybody could well live; there was a neat little creek, where a boat might lie as snug as a puffin in her nest, and out from this creek a ledge of sunken rocks ran into the sea. Now when the Atlantic, according to custom, was raging with a storm, and a good westerly wind was blowing strong on the coast, many a richly laden ship went to pieces on these rocks; and then the fine bales of cotton and tobacco, and such-like things, and the pipes of wine, and the puncheons of rum, and the casks of brandy, and the kegs of Hollands that used to come ashore! Dunbeg Bay was just like a little estate to the Dohertys.

Not but they were kind and humane to a distressed sailor, if ever one had the good luck to get to land; and many a time indeed did Jack put out in his little *corragh* (which, though not quite equal to honest Andrew Hennessy's canvas life-boat, would breast the billows like any gannet), to lend a hand towards bringing off the crew from a wreck. But when the ship had gone to pieces, and the crew were all lost, who would blame Jack for picking up all he could find?

'And who is the worse of it?' said he. 'For as to the king, God bless him! everybody knows he's rich enough already without getting what's floating in the sea.'

Jack, though such a hermit, was a good-natured, jolly fellow. No other, sure, could ever have coaxed Biddy Mahony to quit her father's snug and warm house in the middle of the town of Ennis, and to go so many miles off to live among the rocks, with the seals and sea-gulls for next door neighbours. But Biddy knew that Jack was the man for a woman who wished to be comfortable and happy; for, to say nothing of the fish, Jack had the supplying of half the gentlemen's houses of the country with the *Godsends* that came into the bay. And she was right in her choice; for no woman ate, drank, or slept better, or made a prouder appearance at chapel on Sundays, than Mrs. Dogherty.

Many a strange sight, it may well be supposed, did Jack see, and many a strange sound did he hear, but nothing daunted him. So far was he from being afraid of Merrows, or such beings, that the very first wish of his heart was to fairly meet with one. Jack had heard that they were mighty like Christians, and that luck had always come out of an acquaintance with them. Never, therefore, did he dimly discern the Merrows moving along the face of the waters in their robes of mist, but he made direct for them; and many a scolding did Biddy, in her own quiet way, bestow upon Jack for spending his whole day out at sea, and bringing home no fish. Little did poor Biddy know the fish Jack was after!

It was rather annoying to Jack that, though living in a place where the Merrows were as plenty as lobsters, he never could get a right view of one. What vexed him more was that both his father and grandfather had often and often seen them; and he even remembered hearing, when a child, how his grandfather, who was the first of the family that had settled down at the creek, had been so intimate with a Merrow that, only for fear of vexing the priest, he would have had him stand for one of his children. This, however, Jack did not well know how to believe.

Fortune at length began to think that it was only right that Jack should know as much as his father and grandfather did. Accordingly, one day when he had strolled a little farther than usual along the coast to the northward, just as he turned a point, he saw something, like to nothing he had ever seen before, perched upon a rock at a little distance out to sea: it looked green in the body, as well as he could discern at that distance, and he would have sworn, only the thing was impossible, that it had a cocked hat in its hand. Jack stood for a good half-hour straining his eyes and wondering at it, and all the time the thing did not stir hand or foot. At last Jack's patience was quite worn out, and he gave a loud whistle and a hail, when the Merrow (for such it was) started up, put the cocked hat on its head, and dived down, head foremost, from the rock.

Jack's curiosity was now excited, and he constantly directed his steps towards the point; still he could never get a glimpse of the sea-gentleman with the cocked hat; and with thinking and thinking about the matter, he began at last to fancy he had been only dreaming. One very rough day, however, when the sea was running mountains high, Jack Dogherty determined to give a look at the Merrow's rock (for he had always chosen a fine day before), and then he saw the strange thing cutting capers upon the top of the rock, and then diving down, and then coming up, and then diving down again.

Jack had now only to choose his time (that is, a good blowing day), and he might see the man of the sea as often as he pleased. All this, however, did not satisfy him — 'much will have more —' he wished now to get acquainted with the Merrow, and even in this he succeeded. One tremendous blustering day, before he got to the point whence he had a view of the Merrow's rock, the storm came on so furiously that Jack was obliged to take shelter in one of the caves which are so numerous along the coast; and there, to his astonishment, he saw sitting before him a thing with green hair, long green teeth, a red nose, and pig's eyes. It had a fish's tail, legs with scales on them, and short arms like fins: it wore no clothes, but had the cocked hat under its arm, and seemed engaged thinking very seriously about something.

Jack, with all his courage, was a little daunted; but now or never, thought he: so up he went boldly to the cogitating fishman, took off his hat, and made his best bow.

'Your servant, sir,' said Jack.

'Your servant, kindly, Jack Dogherty,' answered the Merrow.

'To be sure, then, how well your honour knows my name!' said Jack.

'Is it I not know your name, Jack Dogherty? Why, man, I knew your grandfather long before he was married to Judy Regan your grandmother! Ah, Jack, Jack, I was fond of that grandfather of yours; he was a mighty worthy man in his time: I never met his

match above or below, before or since, for sucking in a shellful of brandy. I hope, my boy,' said the old fellow, with a merry twinkle in his little eyes, 'I hope you're his own grandson!'

'Never fear me for that,' said Jack; 'if my mother had only reared me on brandy, 'tis myself that would be a sucking infant to this hour!'

'Well, I like to hear you talk so manly; you and I must be better acquainted, if it were only for your grandfather's sake. But, Jack, that father of yours was not the thing! he had no head at all.'

'I'm sure,' said Jack, 'since your honour lives down under the water, you must be obliged to drink a power to keep any heat in you in such a cruel, damp, *could* place. Well, I've often heard of Christians drinking like fishes: and might I be so bold as to ask where you get the spirits?'

'Where do you get them yourself, Jack?' said the Merrow, twitching his red nose between his forefinger and thumb.

'Hubbubboo,' cries Jack, 'now I see how it is; but I suppose, sir, your honour has got a fine dry cellar below to keep them in.'

'Let me alone for the cellar,' said the Merrow, with a knowing wink of his left eye.

'I'm sure,' continued Jack, 'it must be mighty well worth the looking at.'

'You may say that, Jack,' said the Merrow; 'and if you meet me here, next Monday, just at this time of the day, we will have a little more talk with one another about the matter.'

Jack and the Merrow parted the best friends in the world. On Monday they met, and Jack was not a little surprised to see that the Merrow had two cocked hats with him, one under each arm.

'Might I take the liberty to ask, sir,' said Jack, 'why your honour has brought the two hats with you to-day? You would not, sure, be going to give me one of them, to keep for the *curosity* of the thing?'

14

'No, no, Jack,' said he, 'I don't get my hats so easily, to part with them that way; but I want you to come down and dine with me, and I brought you the hat to dive with.'

'Lord bless and preserve us!' cried Jack, in amazement, 'would you want me to go down to the bottom of the salt sea ocean? Sure I'd be smothered and choked up with the water, to say nothing of being drowned! And what would poor Biddy do for me, and what would she say?'

'And what matter what she says, you *pinkeen?* Who cares for Biddy's squalling? It's long before your grandfather would have talked in that way. Many's the time he stuck that same hat on his head, and dived down boldly after me; and many's the snug bit of dinner and good shellful of brandy he and I have had together below, under the water.'

'Is it really, sir, and no joke?' said Jack; 'why, then, sorrow from me for ever and a day after, if I'll be a bit worse man nor my grandfather was! Here goes — but play me fair now. Here's neck or nothing!' cried Jack.

'That's your grandfather all over,' said the old fellow; 'so come along, then, and do as I do.'

They both left the cave, walked into the sea, and then swam a piece until they got to the rock. The Merrow climbed to the top of it, and Jack followed him. On the far side it was as straight as the wall of a house, and the sea beneath looked so deep that Jack was almost cowed.

'Now, do you see, Jack,' said the Merrow: 'just put this hat on your head, and mind to keep your eyes wide open. Take hold of my tail, and follow after me, and you'll see what you'll see.'

In he dashed, and in dashed Jack after him boldly. They went and they went, and Jack thought they'd never stop going. Many a time did he wish himself sitting at home by the fireside with Biddy. Yet, where was the use of wishing now, when he was so many miles as he thought below the waves of the Atlantic? Still he held hard by the Merrow's tail, slippery as it was; and, at last, to Jack's great surprise, they got out of the water, and he actually found himself on dry land at the bottom of the sea. They landed just in front of a nice house that was slated very neatly with oyster shells! and the Merrow, turning about to Jack, welcomed him down.

Jack could hardly speak, what with wonder, and what with being out of breath with travelling so fast through the water. He looked about him and could see no living things, barring crabs and lobsters, of which there were plenty walking leisurely about on the sand. Overhead was the sea like a sky, and the fishes like birds swimming about in it.

'Why don't you speak, man?' said the Merrow: 'I dare say you had no notion that I had such a snug little concern here as this? Are you smothered, or choked, or drowned, or are you fretting after Biddy, eh?'

'Oh! not myself, indeed,' said Jack, showing his teeth with a good-humoured grin; 'but who in the world would ever have thought of seeing such a thing?'

'Well, come along and let's see what they've got for us to eat?'

Jack really was hungry, and it gave him no small pleasure to perceive a fine column of smoke rising from the chimney, announcing what was going on within. Into the house he followed the Merrow, and there he saw a good kitchen, right well provided with everything. There was a noble dresser, and plenty of pots and pans, with two young Merrows cooking. His host then led him into the room, which was furnished shabbily enough. Not a table or a chair was there in it; nothing but planks and logs of wood to sit on, and eat off. There was, however, a good fire blazing on the hearth — a comfortable sight to Jack.

'Come now, and I'll show you where I keep — you know what,' said the Merrow, with a sly look; and opening a little door, he led

Jack into a fine cellar, well filled with pipes and kegs, and hogs-heads, and barrels.

'What do you say to that, Jack Dogherty? Eh! may be a body can't live snug under the water?'

'Never the doubt of that,' said Jack, with a convincing smack of his under lip, that he really thought what he said.

They went back to the room, and found dinner laid. There was no table-cloth, to be sure — but what matter? It was not always Jack had one at home. The dinner would have been no discredit to the first house of the country on a fast day. The choicest of fish, and no wonder, was there. Turbots, and sturgeons, and soles, and lobsters, and oysters, and twenty other kinds, were on the planks at once, and plenty of the best of foreign spirits. The wines, the old fellow said, were too cold for his stomach.

Jack ate and drank till he could eat no more; then, taking up a shell of brandy, 'Here's to your honour's good health, sir,' said he; 'though, begging your pardon, it's mighty odd that as long as we've been acquainted I don't know your name yet.'

'That's true, Jack,' replied he; 'I never thought of it before, but better late than never. My name's Coomara.'

'And a mighty decent name it is,' cried Jack, taking another shellful: 'here's to your good health, Coomara, and may you live these fifty years to come!'

'Fifty years!' repeated Coomara; 'I'm obliged to you, indeed! If you had said five hundred, it would have been something worth the wishing.'

'By the laws, sir,' cries Jack, '*youz* live to a powerful age here under the water! You knew my grandfather, and he's dead and gone better than these sixty years. I'm sure it must be a healthy place to live in.'

'No doubt of it; but come, Jack, keep the liquor stirring.'

Shell after shell did they empty, and to Jack's exceeding surprise, he found the drink never got into his head, owing, I suppose, to the sea being over them, which kept their noddles cool.

Old Coomara got exceedingly comfortable, and sung several songs; but Jack, if his life had depended on it, never could remember more than

> Rum fum boodle boo,
>   Ripple dipple nitty dob;
> Dumdoo doodle coo,
>   Raffle taffle chittibob!

It was the chorus to one of them; and to say the truth, nobody that I know has ever been able to pick any particular meaning out of it; but that, to be sure, is the case with many a song now-a-days.

At length said he to Jack, 'Now, my dear boy, if you follow me, I'll show you my *curosities!*' He opened a little door and led Jack into a large room, where Jack saw a great many odds and ends that Coomara had picked up at one time or another. What chiefly took his attention, however, were things like lobster-pots ranged on the ground along the wall.

'Well, Jack, how do you like my *curosities?*' said old Coo.

'Upon my *sowkins*, sir,' said Jack, 'they're mighty well worth the looking at; but might I make so bold as to ask what these things like lobster-pots are?'

'Oh! the Soul Cages, is it?'

'The what? sir!'

'These things here that I keep the souls in.'

'*Arrah!* what souls, sir?' said Jack in amazement; 'sure the fish have got no souls in them?'

'Oh! no,' replied Coo, quite coolly, 'that they have not; but these are the souls of drowned sailors.'

'The Lord preserve us from all harm!' muttered Jack, 'how in the world did you get them?'

'Easily enough: I've only, when I see a good storm coming on, to set a couple of dozen of these, and then, when the sailors are drowned and the souls get out of them under the water, the poor things are almost perished to death, not being used to the cold; so they make into my pots for shelter, and then I have them snug, and fetch them home, and keep them here dry and warm; and is it not well for them, poor souls, to get into such good quarters?'

Jack was so thunderstruck he did not know what to say, so he said nothing. They went back into the dining-room, and had a little more brandy, which was excellent, and then, as Jack knew that it must be getting late, and as Biddy might be uneasy, he stood up, and said he thought it was time for him to be on the road.

'Just as you like, Jack,' said Coo, 'but take a *deoch an dorais* before you go; you've a cold journey before you.'

Jack knew better manners than to refuse the parting glass. 'I wonder,' said he, 'will I be able to make out my way home?'

'What should ail you,' said Coo, 'when I'll show you the way?'

Out they went before the house, and Coomara took one of the cocked hats, and put it upon Jack's head the wrong way, and then lifted him up on his shoulder that he might launch him up into the water.

'Now,' says he, giving him a heave, 'you'll come up just in the same spot you came down in; and, Jack, mind and throw me back the hat.'

He canted Jack off his shoulder, and up he shot like a bubble — whirr, whirr, whiz — away he went up through the water, till he came to the very rock he had jumped off, where he found a landing-place, and then in he threw the hat, which sunk like a stone.

The sun was just going down in the beautiful sky of a calm summer's evening. *Feascor* was seen dimly twinkling in the cloudless heaven, a solitary star, and the waves of the Atlantic flashed in a golden flood of light. So Jack, perceiving it was late, set off home; but when he got there, not a word did he say to Biddy of where he had spent his day.

The state of the poor souls cooped up in the lobster-pots gave Jack a great deal of trouble, and how to release them cost him a great deal of thought. He at first had a mind to speak to the priest about the matter. But what could the priest do, and what did Coo care for the priest? Besides, Coo was a good sort of an old fellow, and did not think he was doing any harm. Jack had a regard for him too, and it also might not be much to his own credit if it were known that he used to go dine with Merrows. On

the whole, he thought his best plan would be to ask Coo to dinner, and to make him drunk, if he was able, and then to take the hat and go down and turn up the pots. It was first of all necessary, however, to get Biddy out of the way; for Jack was prudent enough, as she was a woman, to wish to keep the thing secret from her.

Accordingly, Jack grew mighty pious all of a sudden, and said to Biddy that he thought it would be for the good of both of their souls if she was to go and take her rounds at Saint John's Well, near Ennis. Biddy thought so too, and accordingly off she set one fine morning at day-dawn, giving Jack a strict charge to have an eye to the place. The coast being clear, away went Jack to the rock to give the appointed signal to Coomara, which was throwing a big stone into the water. Jack threw, and up sprang Coo!

'Good morrow, Jack,' said he; 'what do you want with me?'

'Just nothing at all to speak about, sir,' returned Jack, 'only to come and take a bit of dinner with me, if I might make so free as to ask you, and sure I'm now after doing so.'

'It's quite agreeable, Jack, I assure you; what's your hour?'

'Any time that's most convenient to you, sir — say one o'clock, that you may go home, if you wish, with the daylight.'

'I'll be with you,' said Coo, 'never fear me.'

Jack went home, and dressed a noble fish dinner, and got out plenty of his best foreign spirits, enough for that matter to make twenty men drunk. Just to the minute came Coo, with his cocked hat under his arm. Dinner was ready, they sat down, and ate and drank away manfully. Jack, thinking of the poor souls below in the pots, plied old Coo well with brandy, and encouraged him to sing, hoping to put him under the table, but poor Jack forgot that he had not the sea over his own head to keep it cool. The brandy got into it and did his business for him, and Coo reeled off home, leaving his entertainer as dumb as a haddock on a Good Friday.

Jack never woke till the next morning, and then he was in a sad way. ''Tis to no use for me thinking to make that old Rapparee drunk,' said Jack, 'and how in this world can I help the poor souls out of the lobster-pots?' After ruminating nearly the whole day, a thought struck him. 'I have it,' says he, slapping his knee; 'I'll be sworn that Coo never saw a drop of *poteen*, as old as he is, and that's the *thing* to settle him! Oh! then, is not it well that Biddy will not be home these two days yet; I can have another twist at him.'

Jack asked Coo again, and Coo laughed at him for having no better head, telling him he'd never come up to his grandfather.

'Well, but try me again,' said Jack, 'and I'll be bail to drink you drunk and sober, and drunk again.'

'Anything in my power,' said Coo, 'to oblige you.'

At this dinner Jack took care to have his own liquor well watered, and to give the strongest brandy he had to Coo. At last says he, 'Pray, sir, did you ever drink any poteen? — any real mountain dew?'

'No,' says Coo; 'what's that, and where does it come from?'

'Oh, that's a secret,' said Jack, 'but it's the right stuff — never believe me again, if 'tis not fifty times as good as brandy or rum either. Biddy's brother just sent me a present of a little drop, in exchange for some brandy, and as you're an old friend of the family, I kept it to treat you with.'

'Well, let's see what sort of thing it is,' said Coomara.

The *poteen* was the right sort. It was first-rate, and had the real smack upon it. Coo was delighted: he drank and he sung *Rum bum boodle boo* over and over again; and he laughed and he danced, till he fell on the floor fast asleep. Then Jack, who had taken good care to keep himself sober, snapped up the cocked hat — ran off to the rock — leaped in, and soon arrived at Coo's habitation.

All was as still as a churchyard at midnight — not a Merrow old or young was there. In he went and turned up the pots, but nothing did he see, only he heard a sort of a little whistle or chirp as he raised each of them. At this he was surprised, till he recollected what the priests had often said, that nobody living could see the soul, no more than they could see the wind or the air. Having now done all that he could do for them he set the pots as they were before, and sent a blessing after the poor souls to speed them on their journey wherever they were going. Jack now began to think of returning; he put the hat on, as was right, the wrong way; but when he got out he found the water so high over his head that he had no hopes of ever getting up into it, now that he had not old Coomara to give him a lift. He walked about looking for a ladder, but not one could he find, and not a rock was there in sight. At last he saw a spot where the sea hung rather lower than any where else, so he resolved to try there. Just as he came to it, a big cod happened to put down his tail. Jack made a jump and caught hold of it, and the cod, all in amazement, gave a bounce and pulled Jack up. The minute the hat touched the water away Jack was whisked, and up he shot like a cork, dragging the poor cod, that he forgot to let go, up with him, tail foremost. He got to the rock in no time, and without a moment's delay hurried home, rejoicing in the good deed he had done.

But, meanwhile, there was fine work at home; for our friend Jack had hardly left the house on his soul-freeing expedition, when back came Biddy from her soul-saving one to the well. When she entered the house and saw the things lying *thrie-na-helah* on the table before her, — 'Here's a pretty job!' said she; 'that blackguard of mine — what ill-luck I had ever to marry him! He has picked up some vagabond or other, while I was praying for the good of his soul, and they've been drinking all the *poteen* that my own brother gave him, and all the spirits, to be sure, that he was to have sold to his honour.' Then hearing an outlandish kind of grunt, she looked down, and saw Coomara lying under the table. 'The blessed Virgin help me,' shouted she, 'if he has not made a real beast of himself! Well, well, I've often heard of a man making a beast of himself with drink! Oh hone, oh hone — Jack, honey, what will I do with you, or what will I do without you? How can any decent woman ever think of living with a beast?'

With such-like lamentations Biddy rushed out of the house, and was going she knew not where, when she heard the well-known voice of Jack singing a merry tune. Glad enough was Biddy to find him safe and sound, and not turned into a thing that was like neither fish nor flesh. Jack was obliged to tell her all, and Biddy, though she had half a mind to be angry with him for not telling her before, owned that he had done a great service to the poor souls. Back they both went most lovingly to the house, and Jack wakened up Coomara; and perceiving the old fellow to be rather dull, he bid him not be cast down, for 'twas many a good man's case; said it all came of his not being used to the *poteen,* and recommended him, by way of cure, to swallow a hair of the dog that bit him. Coo, however, seemed to think he had had quite enough: he got up, quite out of sorts, and without having the manners to say one word in the way of civility, he sneaked off to cool himself by a jaunt through the salt water.

Coomara never missed the souls. He and Jack continued the best friends in the world, and no one, perhaps, ever equalled Jack at freeing souls from purgatory; for he contrived fifty excuses for getting into the house below the sea, unknown to the old fellow, and then turning up the pots and letting out the souls. It vexed him, to be sure, that he could never see them; but as he knew the thing to be impossible, he was obliged to be satisfied.

Their intercourse continued for several years. However, one morning, on Jack's throwing in a stone as usual, he got no answer. He flung another, and another, still there was no reply. He went away, and returned the following morning, but it was to no purpose. As he was without the hat, he could not go down to see what had become of old Coo, but his belief was, that the old man, or the old fish, or whatever he was, had either died, or had removed away from that part of the country.

(from *Fairy Legends and Traditions of the South of Ireland.*)

Country Under Wave

by ALICE FURLONG

There was once a little child, and he could not learn. It was not his fault. Every summer-eve, and every winter-night, he stood by the knee of his mother, and she said for him the names of the days of the week, and the seasons of the year, and told him how to call the sun and the moon and the stars. She gave him to know that the wheat was sown in one time, and reaped in another; that the oxen drew the plough, and the swift, nimble steed the chariot; that there were seven degrees of folks in the land, and seven orders among the poets, and seven colours to be distributed among the folks and among the poets, according to rank and station. And many other things the mother taught him, standing by her knee. The child listened, and was of attentive mind.

But in the morning, she asked him what was shining in the heavens, and he made answer: 'The moon.'

And she asked him when did men take sickles and go a-reaping, and he said: 'In the season of Bealtaine,' (May which is the early summer season when birds are on the bough, and blossom on the thorn).

And she bade him tell her what animal it was that drew the plough over red, loamy fields, and he answered: 'The swift, nimble horse.' And she questioned him of the seven folks, and the seven orders, and the seven colours, and he had no right understanding concerning any of these.

'Ill-luck is on me, that I am the mother of a fool!' said the poor woman, many a time. Then the child used to steal away to the dim, green orchard, and hide among the mossy trees, and weep. After a time, the mother gave up trying to teach him, and taught his younger brothers and his sister, instead. The boy then took the lowest place at table, and his fare was given him last, and he was, in that homestead, the person held in least respect by men-servants and maids.

There was a wise woman tarrying in the place a day, putting herbs of healing about an ailing cow. She saw the boy, and his fair head hanging, and shame in his eyes.

'What is wrong with this fair-headed lad?' said she.

'The head is wrong with him.' answered the mother of the boy. 'He has no utterance nor understanding. A heavy trouble to me, that! For there was none among my kin and people but had the wisdom and the knowledge fitting for his station.' The wise woman muttered and mumbled to herself.

'Get him the Nuts of Knowledge,' said she, after that.

'I have heard tell of them,' said the mother. 'But hard is their getting.' The brothers and the sister of the child that could not learn stood round about, and listened to the talk between the mother and the wise woman, Dechtera.

'The Nuts of Knowledge, they grow upon the Hazels of Knowledge, over a Well of Enchantment in the Country-under-Wave,' said Dechtera. 'If it be that you desire wisdom for your boy, good woman, you must send there some person to bring the nuts to you.'

The second son, Kian, flung back his hair. He was a proud youth, and full of courage as a ripe apple is full of sweetness.

'Let me be going, that the disgrace may be taken from my mother, and the sons of my mother,' said he. The wise woman fingered her long lip.

'If you would go, 'tis soon you must be going,' she said. 'It is near the Eve of Bealtaine, May Eve, an eve of great witchery. Between the rising and the setting of the moon, that night, the loughs and the seas of Erin become gates of glass that will open to let through any person who seeks the Country-under-Wave. Is this to your mind, my son?'

'It is pleasing to my mind,' said the lad.

'It is well-pleasing to my mind,' said the mother.

The wise woman went on telling them of the way to reach Country-under-Wave.

'He must bid farewell to kith and kin, and go in his loneness to the lough-shore, that night,' she said.

'And when the gates of glass are shut behind him, he must tarry in the Under-water-Land from Bealtaine until Samhain (November) and harvest, when the nuts of the Magic Hazels will ripen to scarlet red. And on the Eve of Samhain, (November Eve) he will draw near the Well of Enchantment, and wait for the dropping of the nuts. He must be swift to stretch the hand, and snatch them as they drop. For the Salmon of Knowledge, he is waiting in the Well, to eat the fruit as it falls. In that hour, a rosy surge rises upon the water, and the Salmon eats, and swims away, swimming all the seas of the round, rolling world. And he has a knowledge of everything that passes, over-seas, and under-seas, and in hidden places, and desert ways. But if this youth let the nuts slip through his fingers, he shall be in the power of Them in the Country-under-Wave.'

'Good are my fingers to catch and hold,' said the boy, Kian.

The wise woman went away to the hills, then, after curing the ailing cow.

Came the Eve of Bealtaine, the night of witchery. The lad said farewell to his house and home, and embraced his brothers and his sister and his mother. He went out alone under the moon, and there was fairy-singing in the wind that night, and over the dewy fields the silver track of fairy feet. He came to the lough shore, and saw the water as gates of glass. He went boldly through and travelled crystal roadways and riverways until he came to the Country-under-Wave.

The grass was greener than emeralds there; the trees were bowers of blossom. A radiant mist was on the mountains. The level plain was more thick with flowers than the sky with stars of a night when there is neither moon nor cloud.

'A better country than my mother's country!' said the youth to himself.

He was walking over a shining pebbly way, until he came to a house. Every plank of the wall was of a different colour to the one beside it; the doors and windows were framed and pillared in wrought gold; the roof was fashioned of plumage so finely spread that it seemed like one feather without parting or division.

People were passing to and fro about this fair house. Noble of mien were they, with hair of the hue of primroses; with eyes sloe-black; the blush of the rosy foxglove on every cheek; the pure whiteness of milk on every brow.

They came in a shining troop to meet Kian, the boy, and they said to him: 'A hundred welcomes before you!'

The lad saluted them. They brought him within the palace, and invited him to abide there for the night. He said he was willing. The time went pleasantly with mirth and music. Soon the lad inquired where was the Well of Enchantment?

'More than a day's journey from this spot,' the lord of the mansion made answer.

On the red dawn of the morrow, the lad took his leave of them. They gave him a fair-woven napkin spun of silk as fine as the web of a spider.

'When there comes upon you hunger or thirst, spread this napkin on the grass and it shall be covered with the choicest of food and drinks,' said the lord of the coloured house.

The lad gave them thanks. 'It is a great country you have of it down here,' he said. The noble people were pleased.

'You never were in its like before,' they said. The boy, Kian, felt his high spirit rise up in him. He was a proud lad, and could not listen to a country being praised over his own. That was no fault. But he spoke a word, and the word was not true.

'As many wonders have I seen in my mother's country, and more,' said he. Then he followed the crystal waterways and road-ways, seeking the Well of Enchantment.

The folks of that mansion were watching him along the way.

'A lie in his mouth in return for our hospitality!' said they one to another.

'Well, let it be so. He is not in our power now, but that may be mended another day.'

The boy followed his road. He was travelling till evening, and he came to the shore of the sea. The sand was in grains of gold, the waves fell with the sound of singing. He beheld white-maned sea-horses race upon the strand, and wonderful people in chariots be-hind the horses. He sat down among the flowers, and he spread the fine-spun napkin, and it was covered with choice food and drinks. He ate his supper, and then looked about to find a place to rest for the night. He saw a fair woman coming towards him, and gave her greeting.

'A hundred welcomes before you, Kian,' said she to him. He wondered how she knew his name.

'You are in want of a resting-place for the night?' said she.

'I want that, among other things,' said the lad.

The fair woman led him to a palace among the rocks. It was finer and better than the first house he had been in, if that were possible. Every person there had a star on the forehead, and flowing pale-gold hair, like the ripple of the foam of the sea. And the clothing of every person was of the tint of waves, blue and green, shifting and changing with their stir and movement.

'This is the house of Manannan Mac Lir, who puts command upon the winds and the storms and the tempests that wreck ships and drown fishers,' said the woman.

The boy remained there that night. Pleasant was the entertain-ment he got in the house of Manannan Mac Lir. On the morn of the morrow, he went forth again to find the Well of Enchantment.

The folks of the house gave him a little bit of a cloak, no bigger than would go over the lad's shoulders: 'When you are in want of a shelter and sleeping-booth for the night, hang this cloak from the first straight twig you pick up from the grass. The twig will be a pillar and the cloak a tent, therewith.'

He gave them thanks, and said: 'Wonders upon wonders! What more can you do down here?' The sea-folks laughed out. They laughed more softly than the sigh of summer waves. They were pleased with the youth.

'You have not fallen in with such people before,' said they. The spirit of the lad rose up. He forgot himself again. He told another lie.

'The foot-boys of the King of Erin are better people,' he said, and followed his journey. The folks of that sea-mansion laughed again. But now their laughter was like the whistle of the wind that bids the storm begin.

'A boast he has instead of thanks for us,' said they. 'Let it remain so. He is not in our power now. That will be mended another day.'

Kian, the boy, abode in the Country-under-Wave while the meadows ripened in his mother's country, and mowers went forth with scythes, and maids

32

tossed the hay. The apple was green and the cherry was red. After that, it drew nigh the harvest, and the apple reddened, and the cherry-tree began to change the hue of its leaves. Down in the Country-under-Wave, the youth was walking to and fro, seeking the Well of Enchantment. The day before the eve of Samhain, he came upon it, in a deep forest, where the wind murmured always and always. He saw the magic hazels, and knew them by the crimson of their fruit. And the nut-cluster drooped over the water of the Well, and leaned to its own rosy shadow beneath.

'Now my journey is ended,' said Kian, the boy.

He hung his cloak from the first twig he met in the green, green grass, and it rose to be a pillar, and the cloak spread to be a tent. He threw his fine-spun napkin upon the flowers, and it was covered with food and drinks. He ate his supper, and he took his rest.

But the people of the first mansion had put a sleeping potion in the drink, and it was long that Kian remained in slumber. All the morning he slept; and the noonday sun saw him sleeping, and the rising moon that night. But just before the midnight he awoke, for he seemed to hear his young sister calling upon him to haste, haste, haste. He ran out in the moonlight, and saw the Well shining, and the magic cluster swaying from the bough.

'It is my time now,' said he.

He stood beside the water, and there was the shimmering salmon, with upturned eye, below. But while he waited, all of a sudden, from the tent behind him came the most woeful crying he had ever heard. He thought it was the voice of his mother, and he turned his head. And then, he heard a splash in the water of the Well of Enchantment. The crying ceased as sudden as it began. It was a high, wild cry of laughter he caught, like the wind at night when tempest is out; and the waters of the Well began to rise in a rosy surge; and there was no cluster hanging to its own shadow, but a fruitless bough.

'Now, ill-luck is upon me!' said Kian, the boy.

The water sank, and the Salmon of Knowledge swam to the seas of the round rolling world. The boy sat down by the brink, and covered his head with his mantle, lest any eye might discern his tears. And as he was thus, a deep sleep fell upon him, like to death itself. Then the people of the coloured mansion, and the sea-folks of the palace of Manannan came round him, and they put a grey flag-stone over him, and left him by the Well.

November eve came and went, and the mother of Kian was looking for his return but he never came. 'I had a bad dream concerning him,' said the little sister, Fedelm. The mother sent for the wise woman on the hill.

'Some mishap has befallen,' said Dechtera. 'I do not know what you had best do, now, except you send the third brother to help him. But you must wait for next May-eve.' The woman of the house made lament and moan.

'For a fool has this trouble fallen,' said she. She drove the eldest boy from her presence, and made him sit with the servants. But little Fedelm wept until, for peace sake, the mother had to let him back to his own place. The poor boy that could not learn was filled with shame.

In due season, came the time of Bealtaine, the eve of witchery. Lugaid, the third of the brothers, went forth, in his loneness. He heard the fairy-talk in the wind, and saw, among the dew, the silver track of the feet of Queens from the Raths. He stepped upon the lough-shore, and the gates of glass stood open, and he went through. Not gleefully he went, but against his will, for he cared for no person in the world but himself; neither for the shame of the fool, nor for the lost, bright boy, nor for the sorrow of his mother.

But he said to himself: 'Bad is it that I must go upon this search. But worse it will be if I stay at home, for our house is full of weep-

ing and misery, and there is no comfort to be had in it.'

He was walking crystal streets and roads until he came to the Country-under-Wave, in like manner to his brother. He beheld the bowers and the flowers, the mist of light upon the mountains. He saw the coloured house, and the noble people in their beauty. They came to him.

'A hundred welcomes before you!' said they. He was too fond of his own comfort to doff his head-dress to them.

'In a strange country, no stranger goes without supper,' he said.

The people whispered among themselves.

They said then: 'If you had not asked it, it would have been given to you.'

They brought him within the palace, and gave him his supper,

full and plenty of all kinds. They kept him there that night.

When morning was come, and the crowing of cocks, and a red sun rising, he said to them: 'Is it far to the Well of Enchantment?'

'It will take you nigh a season to find it,' said they to him. He sighed at that, and the lord of the mansion took pity upon him. He gave him a fine-spun napkin, and told him it would be spread with breakfast, dinner, and supper for him, as long as he remained in that place. The lad bade them joy, and went off. He did not doff his head-dress to the women, and he going.

The noble people were angry. 'A churl this is, no lie,' they said. 'Well, he is not in our power to-day, but that will be mended another day.'

Lugaid went up and down that country. He came to the shore, and the ribbed, yellow sands, and the waves that made music in their splash and fall. The steeds of Manannan Mac Lir raced upon the sea; his chariots glistened; his people were there, in glinting, sheeny garments, all changing from green to blue, and from blue to green again. It was night-fall when the lad beheld them, and no light was abroad but the light from the star on the brow of every one of these strange sea-people. One of them came to him.

'You will be in want of shelter to-night?' she said. The boy had been sleeping in dry places under hedges and southern banks. He felt he would like better the comfort of a bed.

'Shelter is a good thing to a tired person, and the night to be at hand,' he answered. She brought him with her into the palace among the rocks. He sat on a couch made of the down of sea swans; he drank out of a cup that was speckled with great emeralds as the grass of a May morning with beads of dew.

There was reciting of hero-tales, and harping and piping, after the banquet. The lad, Lugaid, was heavy with sleep. He let his head fall down, and snored. 'O, 'tis a churl we have in it!' cried the people of Manannan. 'Throw him out with the calves in the byre!' The fair woman who had spoken first with the boy, took his part.

'Long travel he has put over him,' said she, 'and in the shelter of a house he has not slept for nights upon nights.' They let him be, then, until it was morning.

When the morn of the morrow came, the sea-folks gave him the little cloak.

'A tent it will be for you when you need it,' said they. It was a little grey thing, mean to look at. The lad did not believe in the power of the sea-people. He took the cloak and threw it upon his back, and went away, swaggering, and making faces at them over his shoulder. But as he went, he heard them all begin to talk together, and their voices were like the rising of the far tide.

'It is not in our power to harm him, now,' they were saying; 'but that will be mended another day.'

The young lad abode in that Country-under-Wave until Samhain. Everywhere he went, he kept his eyes open for a sight of his brother. But he asked no questions of anybody. In due time he found the deep forest, and the dark Well, the hazels and the ruddy fruit, leaning to its own shadow.

It was sunset on the eve of Samhain. The boy sat down on the ground, near an old grey flag-stone. He spread the napkin out, and there was an abundance both of food and drink upon it, at that. He ate and drank. But the people of the coloured house had put a sleeping potion into his drink, for on this eve they had power to work spells and charms against mortals. The boy drank then, and a heavy slumber fell upon him, and he was there lying in the dew until midnight drew nigh. He heard in his sleep the voice of his sister, Fedelm.

'O, haste, haste, haste!' said the voice. He rose and ran to the Well of Enchantment. The rosy cluster was loosening from the bough. Lugaid, the boy, stretched his hand, and his eye caught the silver gleam of the Salmon of Knowledge below in the water of the Well. But a gust of hollow wind sprang up, all at once, and blew the leaves of the magic hazels into his eyes. Then he heard the fall of the fruit upon the water, and the crimson surge swelled up with little dim noises, and the Salmon ate the nuts, and swam away to the seas of the round, rolling world.

The deep death-trance fell upon Lugaid. He dropped down beside the Well. The sea-folks, and the people of the coloured mansion came, and put a grey-flag-stone over him and left him by his brother.

The mother waited for her boy's return, but he did not return. 'I saw him in my dream,' said Fedelm, the girl. 'I saw him, and he was in a trance of sleep.' The mother sent for Dechtera, the wise woman.

'Lugaid has gone the way of Kian,' said the poor mother. 'What will I be doing now, with no son left me but a fool?'

'Send the daughter after them,' said Dechtera.

'I will not send the daughter,' said the woman of the house. She kissed and embraced the child, and said that she would not part with her. The boy that could not learn said he would not part with her. The mother blessed him for that, and put him into his own proper place at the head of his father's table. There was peace and sorrow among them until it was May-eve again.

'I will go to my rest early to-night,' said Fedelm, the girl.

They did not know what she had in her mind to do. They let her away to her little bower, to her rest. But she wound a silken curtain about the bed-post, and let herself down through the window. She went over the bawn in the light of the moon, and heard the fairy-women singing in the wind, and saw the glimmer of fairy feet dancing over the honey-dew. She went in her loneness, to the lough-shore, and the gates of glass stood open. She took a quick breath, and leaped through, and travelled the crystal highways and glassy roads until she came to the Country-under-Wave.

She found the lovely meads, thick-set with blossoms; and the embowering trees; she saw the mountain-mist, like silver fleeces spread far and thin. She fared to the coloured mansion with its golden pillars, and met the wise people of that house.

'A hundred welcomes before you, fair maid!' said they to her.

'A hundred tears are falling after me,' said Fedelm. They brought her within, and laid choice foods before her. She ate a little honey and bread, and no more. She asked them to tell her the road to the Well of Enchantment?

'It is more than a month's journey from here,' said they. She rose up then, and said she must be on her way though the night was falling. But they besought her, and craved of her to remain in their company that night, since there was now naught to be seen by the Well but hazels with rosy buds upon them. She waited, then, that night.

In the morning they said to her: 'Here is a napkin. Whenever you are hungry or thirsty spread it on the ground, and it shall hold its full of food and drink.' Fedelm took it, and made them a curtsy.

'Is there anything I may do for ye, in return for this gift?' said she.

'Teach a boy to speak truth,' said the lord of the mansion. 'You will not see us again.'

The girl went her way. She fared north and south. She fared east and west. She came to the green-billowed, foam-ridged, hollow sea. The waves were making a melodious, wandering music. The sea-horses pawed the floor of the ocean, and tossed the surf of the high, towering tide. Man-annan and his people were in their chariots, racing and riding on the watery meads. Little Fedelm stood watching them, and the evening fell, and she was so entranced that she forgot to eat or drink.

Then a fair radiant woman came to her, over the seas. She was more lustrous than the evening star when it hangs over the new moon in a twilight blue sky.

'I saw a face like this before,' said she. 'And I saw such clear bright eyes. Who will this little mortal maiden be?' And she stood before Fedelm, and looked her up and down.

'A maiden on a sad quest,' said the girl. 'The daughter of a sad mother; the sister of a sad brother.' Her tears fell, and left her eyes more clear and bright again. The majestic women brought her into the sea-palace. They made her remain with them for that night. There was music and singing, and they asked her if the same was pleasing.

She answered: 'If one were in mournful mood that harping and those singing voices would be enough to make him forget his sadness, though it were the whole world's burden should be upon him.'

'A well-spoken maiden,' said the sea-folks among themselves. On the morn of the morrow, they gave her the small grey cloak, and knowledge of the use of it.

'What shall I do to repay you for this gift?' said Fedelm, curtsying before them.

'Teach a churl fine manners,' said the sea-folks. 'This is our first and last meeting.'

The girl was in the Country-under-Wave until November eve. She found the dim ever-murmuring wood, and the dark deep Well of Enchantment, and the Magic Hazels. The cluster was scarlet-red, swaying above its shadow in the water. The two grey flag-stones were beside. The girl looked at the first of them. It had a streak of moss down the middle of the top. 'That puts me in mind of the curl on the white forehead of Kian, my brother,' said the maid. 'But it was hair brighter than gold, and this is the old green moss on the old grey flag-stone.'

She went wandering about the lone place, and stood by the second flag-stone. There was a score down the middle of the top.

'That, moreover, puts me in mind of my brother, Lugaid, and the frown he used to have on his brow, a furrow of discontent,' said she, musing.

'But what is this but an old grey stone, and he had a brow fairer than snow.'

After that, the evening fell, and all the murmuring, whispering wind of the woods went into a strange silence. And soon the moon rose, round as an apple, and the stars came out, twinkling and beaming over the dew.

Fedelm ate her supper off the magic napkin, and rested a while beneath the enchanted cloak. She was weary. A sleep fell upon her. But in the slumber she seemed to hear faint voices crying and calling. It went to her heart to hear them; for she knew them as the voices of her two lost brothers. She came to herself at the sound. It was the people of the coloured house made her hear the voices. She walked out upon the brink of the Well of Enchantment.

'I discern a creaking in that bough,' she said. If it had not been that the forest was full of silence, she would not have heard it; but this was the work of the sea-folks, to lay a spell of silence on the leaves, that the girl might know the hour was at hand.

It drew near the midnight, and Fedelm stood upon the brink of the Well, and watched the swaying of the bough, and the magic cluster, crimson-red. She saw below her in the wave a great silver salmon, waiting, with upturned eye. And then, the bough creaked, the stalk snapped, and the nuts, shining like fiery rubies, came dropping down upon the water. But the magic cluster never reached the wave, for Fedelm's little fingers seized it as it fell.

The moment the nuts were in her hand she knew all things. She knew the flag-stone with the streak of moss upon it was her dear brother, Kian, who had told a lie to the people of the coloured mansion. She knew the flag-stone with the furrow was Lugaid, the churlish, selfish brother. And she knew how to break the spell upon the one and the other by shaking the water of the Well of Enchantment over them from her little kind hand.

She did that, and they came into their right shapes, and embraced her, and laughed and cried. She led them out by the crystal waterways and roadways, and the gates of glass. They all went back to their mother's house, and great was the welcome they got there. And the boy that could not learn, he ate the Nuts of Knowledge. From that day, he knew all things, the talking of the wind and the whisper of the reeds and rushes, the call of birds, and the cry of beasts, and there was nothing in the whole wide world hidden from him after that day.

(from *Tales of Fairy Folks, Queens and Heroes*)

Darby Doyle's Voyage to Quebec

One fine morning in May, I took the road from Inchegelagh, and got up to the Cove safe and sound. There I saw lots of ships with big broad boards fastened to ropes, every one of them saying: 'The first vessel for Quebec.' Said I to myself, these are about to run for a wager: this one says she'll be first, and that one says she'll be first. At any rate, I pitched on one that was finely painted, and looked long and slender like a currach on the Shannon. When I went on board to ask the fare, who should come up out of a hole but Ned Flinn, an old townsman of my own.

'Is that you, Ned?' said I. 'Are you going to America?'

'Why, to be sure,' said he, 'I'm mate of the ship.'

'Meat! That's your sort, Ned,' said I. 'Then we'll only want bread. Hadn't I better go and pay my way?'

'You've time enough,' said Ned. 'I'll tell you when we're ready for sea. Leave the rest to me, Darby.'

44

'Give us your hand,' said I. 'You were always a great fellow. For the sake of old times, Ned, we must have a drop.'

So my friend Ned brought me to where there was right good stuff. But when it came to three o'clock, I found myself mighty weak with hunger; I had got the smell of corned beef and cabbage that bowled me over entirely. So I went to the landlady, and said I to her: 'Maybe your ladyship would not think me rude for asking if Ned and myself could get our dinner off that fine hot meat that I got a taste of in my nose?'

'In truth, you can, and welcome,' said she, and she looked mighty pleasant.

So the dish and all arrived.

'That's what I call a good feed,' said I. So we ate and drank away. Many's the squeeze Ned gave my fist, telling me to leave it all to him, and how comfortable he'd make me on the voyage. Day after day we spent together, waiting for the wind, till I found my pockets beginning to grow very light.

At last, he said to me, one day after dinner: 'Darby, the ship will be ready for sea on the morrow — you'd better go aboard, and pay your way.'

'Are you joking, Ned?' said I. 'Sure, you told me to leave it all to you.'

'Ah! Darby,' said he, 'you're taking a rise out of me. Sure enough, you were the lad that was never without a joke — the very priest himself couldn't get over you. But, Darby, there's no joke like the true one. I'll stick to my promise: but Darby, you must pay your way.'

'Oh, Ned,' said I, 'is this the way you're going to treat me, after all? I'm a ruined man: all I could scrape together I spent on you. If you don't do something for me, I'm lost. Is there no place where you could hide me from the Captain?'

'Not a place,' said Ned.

'And where, Ned, is the place I saw you coming up out of?'
'Oh, that was the hold, Darby — where the cargo's stowed.'
'And is there no other place?' said I.
'Oh yes,' said he: 'where we keep the water casks.'
'And Ned,' said I, 'does anyone live down there?'
'Not a mother's soul,' said he.

'And Ned,' said I, 'can't you cram me down there, and give me a heap of straw?'

'Why, Darby,' said he, and he looked mighty pitiful, 'I must try. But mind, Darby, you'll have to hide all day in an empty barrel, and when it comes to my watch, I'll bring you down some food; but if you're discovered it's all over with me, and you'll be put on a desolate island to starve.'

'Oh Ned,' said I, 'leave it all to me — never fear, I'll mind myself.'

When night came on, I got down into the dark cellar, among the barrels. Poor Ned fixed a place in a corner for me to sleep, and every night he brought me down hard black cakes and salt meat. There I lay snug for a whole month.

At last, one night, he said to me: 'Now, Darby, what's to be done? We're within three days sail of Quebec. The ship will be overhauled, and all the passengers' names called over. If you are found, you'll be sold as a slave for your passage money.'

'And is that all that frets you?' said I. 'Can't you leave it all to me? In truth, Ned, I'll never forget your hospitality. But, Ned, what place is outside of the ship?'

'Why, the sea, to be sure,' said he.

'I mean, what is the outside of the ship?'

'Why, Darby,' said he, 'part of it's called the bulwark.'

'And thunder and turf!' said I, 'is it bulls that pull the vessel along?'

'No, nor horses,' said he, 'neither. This is no time for joking. What do you mean to do?'

'Why, I'll tell you, Ned — get me an empty meal bag, a bottle, and a bare ham-bone, and that's all I ask.' Ned looked very oddly at me; but he got them for me anyhow.

'Well, Ned,' said I, 'you know I'm a great swimmer. Your watch will be early in the morning; I'll just slip down into the sea; do you cry out "There's a man in the water!" as loud as you can, and leave all the rest to me.'

Well, to be sure, down into the sea I dropped without as much as a splash. Ned roared out, with the hoarseness of a braying ass: 'A man in the sea! A man in the sea!'

Every man, woman and child came running up out of the holes, the captain among the rest, who put a long red barrel like a gun to his eye — and thinking he was intent on shooting me, down I dived. When I got my head over the water again, what should I

48

see but a boat rowing to me as fast as a trout after a pinkeen. When it came up close enough to be heard, I roared out: 'Bad cess to you, for a set of spalpeen rascals, did you hear me at last?'

The boat now ran upon the top of me; down I dived again like a duck after a frog, but the minute my skull came over the water, I was gripped by the scruff of the neck, and dragged into the boat. To be sure, didn't I kick up a row!

'Let go my hair, you blue devils,' I roared. 'It's well you have

me at your mercy in this desolate place, or by the powers, I'd make you feel the strength of my bones. What hard luck I had to follow you at all; which of you is the master?'

As I said this, every mother's son began to stare at me, with my bag round my neck, and my bottle by my side and the bare bone in my fist.

'There he is,' said they, pointing to a little yellow man in a corner of the boat.

'May bad weather raise blisters on your shins,' said I, 'you yellow-looking monkey, but it's almost time for you to think of letting me into your ship — I'm here ploughing and plunging this month after you. Sure, I didn't care a thrawneen, was it not that you have my best Sunday clothes in your ship, and my name in your books. For three straws, as I don't know how to write, I'd leave my mark, and that on your skull!' So saying, I made a lick at him with the ham-bone, but I was near tumbling into the sea again.

'And pray, what is your name, my lad?' said the Captain.

'What's my name? What would you give to know?' said I, 'you unmannerly spalpeen — it might be what's your name, Darby Doyle, out of your mouth — aye, Darby Doyle, that was never afeared or ashamed to own it, at home or abroad!'

'And Mr Darby Doyle,' said he, 'do you mean to persuade us that you swam from Cork to here, after us?'

'That's more of your ignorance,' said I, 'aye, and if you'd stayed three days longer, and not taken me up, I'd have been in Quebec before you — only my provisions were out, and the few rags of bank-notes I had all melted into paste in my pocket, for I hadn't time to get them changed. But stay, wait till I get my foot on shore, there's never a coroner in Cork if you don't pay for leaving me to the mercy of the waves.'

All this time the blue chaps were pushing the boat with sticks through the water, till at last we came close to the ship. Everyone on board saw me at the Cove, but didn't see me on the voyage; to be sure, everyone's mouth was wide open, crying out, 'Darby Doyle!'

'Shut your throats,' said I, 'it's now you can call me loud enough; you wouldn't shout that way when you saw me rolling like a tub in a mill-race the other day before your faces.'

When they heard me say that, some of them grew pale as a sheet — but the captain does no more but runs to the book, and calls out the names that paid, and them that hadn't paid. To be sure, I was one of them that didn't pay. If the Captain looked at me before with wonderment, he now looked with astonishment! Nothing was talked of for the other three days but Darby Doyle's great swim from the Cove to Quebec.

One said: 'I always knew Darby to be a great swimmer.'

'Do you remember,' said another, 'when Darby's dog was near being drowned in the great duck hunt, and Darby peeled off and brought in the dog, and made after the duck himself, and swam for two hours endways; and do you remember when all the dogs gathered round the duck at one time; when it went down how Darby dived after it, and stayed down for almost an hour — and stayed below while the creature was eating a few frogs, for she was weak and hungry; and when everybody thought he was lost, up he came with the duck by the leg in his left hand?'

I agreed to all they said, till at last we got to America. I was now in a queer way; the captain wouldn't let me go till a friend of his would see me. By this time, not only his friends came, but swarms upon swarms staring at poor Darby. At last I called Ned.

'Ned,' said I, 'I want to go about my business.'

'Be easy, Darby,' said he, 'haven't you your fill of good eating, and the captain's got mighty fond of you entirely.'

51

'Is he, Ned?' said I. 'But tell us, Ned, are all them crowds of people going to sea?'

'No, you amadhaun,' said Ned, 'sure, they are come to look at you.'

Just as he said this, a tall yellow man, with a black curly head, came and stared me full in the face.

'You'll know me again,' said I, 'confound your manners, and the schoolmaster that taught you.' But I thought he was going to shake hands with me, when he took hold of my fist and opened every finger, one by one, then opened my shirt, and looked at my breast.

'Pull away, my boy,' said I, 'I'm no deserter, at any rate.' But never an answer he made me, but walked down into the hole where the captain lived.

'This is more of it,' said I. 'Ned, what could that tallow-faced man mean?'

'Why,' said Ned, 'he was looking to see if your fingers were webbed, or had you scales on your breast.'

'His impudence is great,' said I, 'did he take me for a duck or a bream? But Ned, what's the meaning of the boards across the stick the people walk on, and the big white board up there?'

'Why, come over and read,' said Ned.

But I didn't know whether I was standing on my head or on my heels, when I saw in great big black letters:

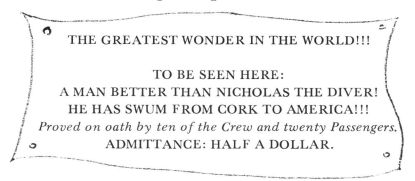

THE GREATEST WONDER IN THE WORLD!!!

TO BE SEEN HERE:
A MAN BETTER THAN NICHOLAS THE DIVER!
HE HAS SWUM FROM CORK TO AMERICA!!!
Proved on oath by ten of the Crew and twenty Passengers.
ADMITTANCE: HALF A DOLLAR.

'Tell me, Ned,' said I, 'does this mean your humble servant?'

'No-one else,' said he. So I made no more ado, but with a hop, skip and jump, got over to the captain, who was now talking to the yellow fellow that was after staring me out of countenance.

'Pardon my rudeness, your honour,' said I, mighty polite, and making a bow. At the same time Ned was at my heels — so raising my foot, to give the genteel scrape I hit his leg and scraped all the skin off his shins.

'To the devil with your brogues,' said he.

'You'd better not curse the wearer,' said I, 'or —'

'Oh, Darby!' said the captain, 'don't be ungenteel, and so many ladies and gentlemen looking at you.'

'The never another mother's soul shall lay their peepers on me

till I see sweet Inchegelagh again,' said I. 'You're doing it well. How much money have you gathered for my swimming?'

'Be quiet, Darby,' said the captain, and he looked very much frightened. 'I have plenty, and I'll have more for you if you do what I want you to do.'

'And what is that?' said I.

'Why, Darby,' said he, 'I'm after holding a wager last night with this gentleman, for all the worth of my ship, that you'll swim against any swimmer in the world; and Darby, if you don't do that, I'm a gone man.'

'Then give me your fist,' said I, 'did you ever hear of the sons of the sod deceiving any man in the European world yet — barring themselves?'

'Well, Darby,' said he, 'I'll give you a hundred dollars; but Darby, you must keep to your word, and you shall have another hundred.'

So saying, he brought me down into the cellar; but I didn't think for the life of me to see such a wonderful place; nothing but gold every way I turned, and Darby's own sweet face in twenty places. I was almost ashamed to ask the gentleman for the dollars. But said I to myself again — the gentleman has too much money! I suppose he does be throwing it into the sea, for I often heard the sea was richer than the land, so I may as well take it, anyhow.

'Now Darby,' said he, 'here's the dollars for you.' But it was only a bit of paper he was handing me.

'None of your tricks upon travellers,' said I, 'I had better than that, and many more of them, melted in the sea; give me what won't wash out of my pocket.'

'Why, Darby,' said he, 'this is an order on a merchant for the amount.'

'I'd sooner take your word than his oath,' said I, looking round mighty respectful at the gold walls.

'Well, well, Darby,' said he, 'you must have the real thing.' So, sure enough, he reckoned me out a hundred dollars in gold. I never saw the like since the stocking fell out of the chimney on my aunt, and cut her forehead.

'Now Darby,' said he, 'you are a rich man, and you are worthy of it all — sit down, Darby, and take a bottle of wine.' So to please the gentleman, I sat down. After a bit, who comes down but Ned.

'Captain,' said he, 'the deck is crowded; I had to block up the gang-way to prevent any more from coming in to see Darby. Bring him up, or sure as a gun, the ship will sink.'

'Come up, Darby,' said the captain, smiling wonderful pleasant at myself. So he handed me up through the hall as tender as if I was a lady, or a pound of fresh butter in the dog-days. When I got up, sure enough, I couldn't help staring; such crowds of fine ladies and yellow gentlemen never was seen before in any ship. One of them, a little rosy-cheeked beauty, whispered the captain some-thing, but he shook his head, and then came over to me.

'Darby,' said he, 'I know an Irishman would do any thing to please a lady.'

'In truth you may say that with your own pretty mouth,' said I.

'That's a good fellow,' said he. 'Now strip off.'

'Decency!' said I, 'is it in my mother-naked pelt

55

before the ladies? Hard fortune to the undescent, brazen-faced —
no matter! Irish girls for ever after that!' But all to no use — I
had to peel off behind a big sheet, and then I made one race,
and jumped ten yards into the water to get out of their sight.
Sure enough, everyone's eyes danced in their head, while they
looked on the spot where I went down. A thought came into my
head while I was below, how I'd show them a little diversion, as I
could use a great many tricks in the water. So I didn't rise at all
till I got to the other side, and everyone ran to that side; then I
took a hold of my two big toes, and making a ring of myself,
rolled like a hoop on the top of the water all round the ship. I
believe I opened their eyes! Then I back swum, and dived, till at
last the captain made signs to me to come out, so I got into the
boat, and threw on my duds. The very ladies were breaking their
necks, running to shake hands with me.

'Sure,' said they, 'you're the greatest man in the world!!' So
for three days I showed off to crowds of people, though I was
frying in the water for shame.

At last the day came. I saw the captain looking very often at
me. At last, 'Darby,' said he, 'are you any way cowed? The fellow
you have to swim against can swim down waterfalls and cataracts.'

'Can he?' said I. 'But can he swim up them? Darby's the one for
that! But captain, come here: are all my provisions ready? Don't
let me fall short of a drop of the real stuff, above all things.'

And who should come up while I was talking to the captain,
but the chap I was to swim with, and heard all I said. His eyes
grew as big as two oyster shells. Then the captain called me aside.

'Darby,' said he, 'do you put on this green jacket and white
trousers, that the people may better distinguish you from the
other chap.'

'With all hearts,' said I. 'Green forever — Darby's own favourite
colour the world over; but where am I going to, captain?'

'To the swimming place, to be sure,' said he.

'Here's at you, my hearty,' said I, 'and the devil take the hindmost.' I was then introduced in due form to the swimmer. I looked at him from head to foot. He was so tall that he could eat bread and butter over my head — with a face as yellow as a kite's foot.

'Tip us the mitten,' said I, quite pleasant. Said I to myself, I'm done - but, cheer up, Darby! If I'm not able to kill him, I'll frighten the life out of him.

'Where are we going to swim to?' said I, though if all was known, I was rightly nonplussed at the same time. But never a word he answered.

'Are you bothered, neighbour?' said I to him again, mighty stiff.

'I reckon I'm not,' said he, as chuff as a bear.

'Well then,' said I, 'why didn't you answer your betters? What would you think if we swam to Cape Clear or the Cape of Good Hope?'

'I reckon neither,' said he again, eyeing me as if I was going to pick his pockets.

'Well then, have you any favourite place?' said I. 'Now, I've heard a great deal about the island where poor Bony died. I'd like to see it, if I had anyone to show me the place; suppose we went there.' But not a taste of a word could I get out of him, good or bad — so off we set through the crowds of ladies and gentlemen. Such cheering and waving of hats never was seen even at Dan's entry into Dublin; and then the row of pretty girls laughing and rubbing up against me, that I could hardly get on. To be sure, no-one could be looking to the ground, and not be looking at them, till at last I was tripped up by a big lump of iron stuck fast in the ground, with a big ring to it.

'Whoo! Darby,' said I, 'making a hop and a crack of my fingers, 'you're not down yet.' I turned round to look at what tripped me.

'What do you call that?' said I to the captain, who was at my elbow.

'Why, Darby,' said he, 'that's half an anchor.'

'Have you any use for it?' said I.

'Not in the least,' said he, 'it's only to fasten boats to.'

'Maybe, you'd give it to a body,' said I.

'And welcome, Darby,' said he, 'it's yours.'

'Good luck to your honour, sir,' said I, 'it's my poor father that will pray for you. When I left home, the creature hadn't as much as an anvil but what was stolen away by the agent — bad luck to him. This will be just the thing that'll match him; he can tie the

horse to the ring, while he forges on the other part. Now, will you oblige me by getting a couple of chaps to lay it on my shoulder when I get into the water, and I won't have to be coming back for it after I shake hands with this fellow.' The chap turned from yellow to white when he heard me say this; and said he to the gentleman that was walking by his side, 'I reckon I'm not fit for the swimming today — I don't feel myself.'

'Send for your brother, then, and I'll wait here till he comes. Here man, take a drop of this before you go. Here's to your better health, and your brother's into the bargain.' So I drank up my glass, and handed him another; but never a drop of it he'd take.

'No-one's forcing you, son,' said I, 'maybe you think there's poison in it?' — and taking another glass myself — 'Well, here's good luck to us, once more. And when will you be able for the swim?' said I, mighty complacent.

'I reckon in another week,' said he.

So we shook hands and parted. The poor fellow went home — took the fever — then began to rave: 'Swim up cataracts! — swim to the Cape of Good Hope! — swim to St Helena! — swim to Cape Clear! — swim with an anchor on his back! Oh! Oh! Oh! that'll never do for me.'

I now thought it best to be on the move; so I gathered up my winnings; and here I sit under my own hickory trees, as independent as any Yankee.

(T.E. from *The Dublin Penny Journal*)

Big Seán

by LADY WILDE

The islanders believe firmly in the existence of fairies who live in the caves by the sea — little men about the height of a sod of turf, who come out of the fissures of the rocks and are bright and merry, wearing green jackets and red caps, and ready enough to help any one they like, though often very malicious if offended or insulted.

There was an old man on the island called Seán-Mor, who said that he had often travelled at night with the little men and carried their sacks for them; and in return they gave him strange fairy gifts and taught him the secret of power, so that he could always triumph over his enemies; and even as to the fairies, he was as wise as any of them, and could fight half a dozen of them together if he were so minded, and pitch them into the sea or strangle them with seaweed. So the fairies were angered at his pride and presumption, and determined to do him a malicious turn, just to amuse themselves when they were up for fun. So one night when he was returning home, he suddenly saw a great river between him and his house.

'How shall I get across now?' he cried aloud; and immediately an eagle came up to him.

'Don't cry, Seán-Mor,' said the eagle, 'but get on my back and I'll carry you safely.'

So Seán-Mor mounted, and they flew right up ever so high, till at last the eagle tumbled him off by the side of a great mountain in a place he had never seen before.

'This is a bad trick you have played me,' said Seán; 'tell me where I am now?'

'You are in the moon,' said the eagle, 'and get down the best way you can, for now I must be off; so good-bye. Mind you don't fall off the edge. Good-bye,' and with that the eagle disappeared.

Just then a cleft in the rock opened, and out came a man as pale as the dead with a reaping-hook in his hand.

'What brings you here?' said he. 'Only the dead come here,' and he looked fixedly at Seán-Mor so that he trembled like one already dying.

'O your worship,' he said, 'I live far from here. Tell me how I am to get down, and help me I beseech you.'

'Ay, that I will,' said the pale-faced man. 'Here is the help I give you,' and with that he gave him a blow with the reaping-hook which tumbled Seán right over the edge of the moon; and he fell and fell ever so far till luckily he came in the midst of a flock of geese, and the old gander that was leading stopped and eyed him.

'What are you doing here, Seán-Mor?' said he, 'for I know you well. I've often seen you down in Shark. What will your wife say

when she hears of your being out so late at night, wandering about in this way. It is very disreputable, and no well brought up gander would do the like, much less a man; I am ashamed of you, Seán-Mor.'

'O your honour,' said the poor man, 'it is an evil turn of the evil witches, for they have done all this; but let me just get up on your back, and if your honour brings me safe to my own house I shall be for ever grateful to every goose and gander in the world as long as I live.'

'Well then, get up on my back,' said the bird, fluttering its wings with a great clatter over Seán; but he couldn't manage at all to get on its back, so he caught hold of one leg, and he and the gander went down and down till they came to the sea.

'Now let go,' said the gander, 'and find your way home the best way you can, for I have lost a great deal of time with you already, and must be away;' and he shook off Seán-Mor, who dropped plump down into the sea, and when he was almost dead a great whale came sailing by, and flapped him all over with its fins. He knew no more till he opened his eyes lying on the grass in his own field by a great stone, and his wife was standing over him drenching him with a great pail of water, and flapping his face with her apron.

And then he told his wife the whole story, which he said was true as gospel, but I don't think she believed a word of it, though she was afraid to let on the like to Seán-Mor, who affirms to this day that it was all the work of the fairies, though wicked people might laugh and jeer and say he was drunk.

(from *Ancient Legends, Mystic Charms
and Superstitions of Ireland*)

The
Water
Witch

I n the vicinity of the ferry, which is near a mile across, between Youghal and the County Waterford, lived an old woman, whose tottering gait and wrinkled visage, joined to habits of seclusion and loneliness, had procured for her the appellation of 'The Water Witch.'

Though her hut joined other houses, chiefly belonging to boatmen, yet few had the hardihood, after nightfall, to loiter near her domicile, where she sat in the chim-ney-corner, before the glimmering light of a few dried sticks, or faggots, which she picked up in her rambles. Not only her own immediate neighbours, but many others also, even to the most remote parts of the town, had their remarks to pass about Gummer Sampson.

When she came in among them they could not exactly tell; but she could be no good body certainly,

63

for she had no occupation that they could see — and how did she contrive to live? And then, she was all alone; she never visited, and she never asked a soul to darken her doors. Curiosity and conjecture were busy upon all these points, but the only conclusion they could come to was — she must be a witch!

This point once settled, there were not wanting dark and frightful stories of her midnight incantations, and the company she entertained when the rest of the neighbours were asleep. In the wildest and most tempestuous weather it was said she took the greatest delight; but not like others of her dreaded sisterhood, to ride away through the angry clouds on a broomstick; — no, the water — the foaming waves of the sea was her element, and her pleasure-yacht no other than a cockle-shell.

She knew when a storm was approaching, and putting down a pot of eggs, the old hag would sit watching it, and according as they would break and mount to the top, she would say with a devilish grin, 'There's one! — that's another gone! — Hark! poor wretches, how they shriek! — in vain — down, down they sink into their yawning grave!'

Jack Linehan and Bill Carty were as light-hearted and laughter-loving souls as ever cracked a joke, or sung a good song over the flowing can, or merrily footed it to the joyous sound of the bag-pipes; and, withal, they were set down by the old fishermen, as being two of the most expert and steady fellows that ever handled an oar, or trimmed a sail. Fearless and fond of fun they would watch old Gummer Sampson as she hobbled out in search of her daily food and firing, and they would laugh at her, and ask her when she intended to have company next, that they might be of the party, or when she would go cruising in her cockle-shell, that they might have a sail with her.

Sometimes they would nail up her door in her absence, and feel delighted at her distress; while she, shaking her thin grey locks, would mutter between her teeth, and the more serious people would advise them not to meddle with the old woman, or they may rue the consequences. Jack Linehan and Bill Carty were, therefore, it may be presumed, no favourites with Gummer Sampson.

One night that they were returning home late, with a few more from a christening, their laughter loud and long, and their eyes dancing in their heads from the exhilarating effects of the bottle, they proposed paying a visit to the old Witch. As they approached her hut, those that had set out with them dropped off one by one, their natural desire of prying melting away, like brass in the furnace, before the soul-harrowing image of the wrinkled hag at her midnight orgies; and as they stood before her door they were alone. What they saw and heard then was never known; but they did not appear to be the same persons after, so completely were they changed. When rallied by their friends as to their visit that night, and what they saw, they strove to laugh it off, but the sound of their own heartless voices startled even themselves, and seemed more like the hollow mockery of the echoing charnel-house, than the clear-toned merriment of former days.

On the evening after this occurrence, Jack Linehan and his mother were sitting at their little fire, repairing a fishing-net, and she trying, at the same time, with all the ingenuity of an adept in the art of fishing for secrets, to get Jack's out of his bosom by hook or by crook, but all in vain; there it lay as deep as if it were at the bottom of the ocean.

He at last silenced all further enquiries by saying, in a solemn tone, while his cheek turned to an ashy hue, 'For the love of God, mother, don't ask me any more about it; I cannot tell you now what I saw and heard, perhaps when I return home to-morrow evening I may, but you must promise (and he lowered his voice) never, while the breath is in your body, to repeat it again to a living soul!'

The first grey dawn of the morning had scarcely begun to dim the lustre of the twinkling stars, when Jack and Bill were seen hastening down to the quay, and were soon busily engaged getting in their nets and trimming the sails of their fishing-smack, of which they were joint-owners. There was one young boy with them who generally accompanied them. The anchor was in — the rope coiled — they got clear of the boats around them, which were also preparing to start, and dipping their oars into the water, dropped quietly out, the first that left the quay-wall. The other fishermen remarked that they never saw 'The Sisters' creep away from them so silently before; they missed the joyous shout and the hearty salute that were wont to greet their ears, and heard not the merry glees borne back upon the wind as they stood out to sea.

The day was fine, and as 'The Sisters' cut her swift way through the waters, the spirits of Jack Linehan and Bill Carty revived once more; and they appeared to forget that awful night's adventure the more they left the scene of it behind. But as the evening set in, dark clouds were seen gathering, the wind sung in fitful moanings through the cordage; and then the old and more experienced fishermen, as they steered their boats homewards through the swelling brine, foretold a stormy night. The last of the fishing-smacks had long past 'The Sisters' ere her owners commenced hauling in their nets; and when Jack took the helm and cried out to his companions to 'stand by,' the breeze, which had been every moment freshening, had increased to a tremendous gale of wind. The sea had become awfully convulsed. Now lifted upon a mountainy wave, then plunging into the yawning gulf, it required all the art and steadiness that the young fishermen were possessed of to keep their little boat from perishing. The words they exchanged were but few; it was no time, and they were in no mood for conversation. Jack, with his hand firmly grasped on the tiller, was intently looking out a-head.

Bill was minding the sails, and the boy with trembling haste was bailing out the water, when suddenly Jack sung out — his head bent forwards, and his eyes starting from their sockets, 'Look out a-head!'

They did so; and right before them, riding upon the waves, they perceived something, but could not plainly distinguish what, apparently approaching them.

At last Bill exclaimed — 'Holy queen of heaven! it is the Witch!'

And the next moment Gummer Sampson was at their side, seated in her cockle-shell. A fiendish grin lit up her shrivelled features, as her croaking voice was heard above the roaring of the tempest.

'Ha! ye persecuting dogs, are ye there? Ye wished to meet me on the waters, and ye have your wish. Where is your insulting laugh now? Ye were merry with the poor helpless old woman on the dry land, but it is my turn now to laugh at ye upon the stormy ocean — Ha! ha! ha ha!' — and her devilish voice rose upon the wind, and seemed to penetrate through all the chambers of the deep.

While it was yet ringing in the ears of the hapless horror-stricken fishermen, Jack's powerless hand dropped from the tiller — a wave struck the boat, and she filled instantly. A shriek of despair burst from them — the old hag laughed still louder.

'Ye will tell what ye saw and heard that night, won't ye? — aye, to the fishes. — Ha! ha! ha!' — and the waves closed above 'The Sisters' and her little crew.

One rose, it was the boy; and while he closed his eyes at the horrible vision before him, he still gasped and struggled for life.

'You never injured me nor mine,' said the old woman, in a

subdued tone.

'The innocent may not perish with the guilty. — Cling to that oar, firmly. — Fear not, but hold on for your life;' and the boy grasped at the oar which was floating by his side.

When he looked again the hag was gone — the sea was calmer, and he felt himself borne along at a swift rate.

On the following morning, as a few people were hurrying along the strand, near Clay-Castle, on their way to town, they perceived something lying extended, which, on a nearer approach, they found to be a shipwrecked sailor, an oar held firmly in his grasp. They thought him dead at first, but on raising him the signs of life were visible, and they conveyed him to the nearest dwelling.

When he recovered they could not collect from him where he came from, or what ship he belonged to; the only answer he could make to their enquiries was a laugh; and pointing forward, he would cry out, 'There she is! There she is!'

'Poor boy,' said they, 'his brain is turned through grief and fright. It was a fearful night, and perhaps he saw all his friends perishing before him.'

The loss of 'The Sisters' soon spread around, and cast a gloom over the little town. The people who first saw the shipwrecked boy mentioned the circumstance, and his friends immediately hurried out and brought him home; but he never came to his senses rightly again. One thing the neighbours thought very extraordinary, and it was with many a solemn shrug and shake of the head they remarked it to each other — old Gummer Sampson did not make her appearance after the night of 'The Sisters' being lost. The fishermen, calling a council, came to the determination of pulling down her hut, which they soon accomplished, and burned and destroyed every article in it.

It was many days after this when the poor brain-cracked boy recovered sufficiently to relate the awful and soul-sickening occur-

rences of that long-remembered night; it made a deep impression upon the minds of the good people of Youghal, but they never laid their eyes again upon the wrinkled visage and stooping figure of 'The Water Witch!'

(G.C. from *The Irish Penny Magazine*)

The Adventures of Ciad

by SEAMUS MACMANUS

Ciad, Ceud, and Mith-Ceud were the three sons of the King of Norway. All over the world they were celebrated as fine, brave fellows, and they had come to think themselves so, too.

On a day after Ciad had been walking by the shore for a long time, thinking, he came back to his father's castle.

He said to his father and his brothers: 'Ceud and Mith-Ceud and Ciad are celebrated far and wide as great heroes and gallant champions, but I have just been thinking, do we deserve this? Neither of us has ever done anything great. I think it is not right to bear the name of champion without having done something to earn it. I will leave my father's castle, and go away and prove my right to the title of hero, or, if I fail, I will never come back.'

The King of Norway tried hard to persuade him not to go, but Ciad would not be persuaded.

He said: 'I am sorely ashamed of myself for bearing a title that I have not deserved.'

Then, when the King found that Ciad was bent on going, he asked him to take the pick of his men to accompany him on his adventures.

'No, I'll go by myself,' said Ciad.

The King could not induce him to take any men.

Early next morning Ciad was up and breakfasted. He took his arms and his shield with him, and started off. He went to the seashore, and travelled away and away, along it.

When he had been travelling for three hours, he saw a speck far out at sea, but it was coming nearer and getting bigger every minute. At last he saw it was a boat, and when it came still nearer, he saw that a woman sat in it. When it was nearer still, he saw that she was a very beautiful lady.

He stood his ground, as the boat was coming straight toward him. At length the boat's keel grated on the gravel, and Ciad helped the young lady on shore.

'Beautiful lady, who are you? Where do you come from? Or where do you go all alone?' he said.

'Before I answer that,' she said, 'give me your name; for I will not reply to those questions unless you are of royal blood.'

'I am of royal blood. I am Ciad, son of the King of Norway,' he said.

She said: 'I am glad of that. I am Dark Eye, the daughter of the King of France. From France I have come, but where I am going I do not know. For a year and a day I have been wandering over the seas in this little boat, seeking for a champion. A cruel step-mother has laid a spell on me, under which I have to leave home, and must wander forever and ever over the seas and the oceans

in this little boat, unless I can find for her the bottle of loca
[loca was a balm that could instantly cure all wounds, and even
restore life itself to the dead] that is owned by the Queen of the
Island of the Riches of the World. When I find that, my step-
mother's spell will be lifted off me. For three years now I have
been wandering over the world seeking for this island, but cannot
find it, and can find no one who knows where it is. I have already
put geasa on the twelve greatest champions of the world, ordering
them to bring me this bottle. None of them got it, but instead
the twelve lost their lives. As you are a King's son and a hero,
I put geasa upon you to bring me this bottle of loca of the Queen
of the Island of the Riches of the World, and hand it to me on this
spot in three years and a day from now.

Ciad said: 'I accept the geasa, Dark Eye.'

Dark Eye thanked him. He helped her into her boat; she pushed off, and sailed away and away until he lost sight of her. Then Ciad turned and walked back to his father's castle. He told his father of his adventure and of the geasa that had been laid on him.

'My poor boy,' his father said, 'I am very sorry for you. There are not three in all the world who know where the Island of the Riches of the World is, and even if you could find that, you would lose your life in trying to take the bottle of loca.'

Ciad said that better men than he had already lost their lives in the search, so it would be no shame for him if he, too, lost his.

His father asked him to take nine times nine nines of men with him, if he was bent on fulfilling his geasa.

But Ciad said: 'No. I shall not take nine men. Give me a ship, and let my brothers Ceud and Mith-Ceud go along with me. If it is possible to get the bottle of loca of the Queen of the Island of the Riches of the World, I with Ceud and Mith-Ceud, will get it. If it is impossible then your nine times nine nines of men would be lost to you, as well as we.'

His father gave him the best ship in the harbour, and with Ceud and Mith-Ceud, Ciad, on the morrow, set out on his quest.

They sailed for two days and two nights without meeting any adventure; and on the third day they saw a speck on the sea, far off. Very soon they saw it was a ship coming towards them. As they came nearer to it they found that it was very large, and when they came very near they saw that in the ship was one person, a great giant, greater than any giant in Norway.

When the strange ship came up beside them, the giant asked Ciad who he was and what right he had to sail these waters.

Ciad said: 'My name I'm not ashamed of. I am Ciad, the son of the King of Norway, a hero. Who are you, and by what right do you question me?'

He said: 'I am the Giant of the Great Seas, and I allow no ship upon these waters.'

Said Ciad: 'If that is your law I am sorry for you, for it's going to be broken this day.'

The giant raised his spear, and Ciad, without waiting, leaped aboard the giant's ship with his spear in his hand and with his shield before him.

Ciad and the Giant of the Great Seas fell to, and fought as two men never fought before. Their fight was so loud and so fierce and so terrible that the seals came from the North Seas and the whales came from the deeps of the ocean, and the little red fishes came up from the sea-meadows and gathered around the ships to watch the fight. The giant was brave and a great fighter, without doubt; his strength and skill were wonderful; but the courageous spirit of Ciad was greater than the giant's strength and skill. When the sun was two hours above the Eastern waters they had begun the fight, and when it was going down into the Western waters the fight was not ended. But it was very nearly so, for the giant was weakening, and soon he would have been beaten, but he gave three calls, and a blue mist came down from the skies and wrapped his ship round.

When the mist cleared away, the giant and the ship were gone, and Ciad was struggling in the water.

Ceud and Mith-Ceud took him aboard and found he was so badly abused and so weak from fighting and loss of blood, that there was nothing for it but to return home; so home they went.

At home Ciad lay in his bed for three days, with his father's doctors attending him. At the end of that time he got up and asked his father to give him thirty men and another ship, that he might set out on his journey again.

His father tried to persuade him not to go, but it was of no use. Ciad said if he did not fulfill his geasa, he could never hold up his head with men again.

Then he set out with two ships. Ceud, Mith-Ceud, and himself were in one ship, and his father's thirty men in the other.

They sailed for three days and three nights in the same direction in which they had gone before, and on the morning of the fourth day, he saw two specks on the waters, far off. They were coming towards him. They got larger every moment. He saw they were two ships. When they came nearer, he saw the giant standing in one, and a host of men in the other. When they came quite close, Ciad hailed the Giant of the Great Seas and asked him did he mean battle.

The giant replied: 'If you do not mean battle, I do not.'

'Where are you going then?' Ciad asked.

The giant said: 'I'm going in search of the Riches of the World.'

'Where is that to be found?' said Ciad.

'It's on an island in the Far World,' the giant said, 'and is owned by the Queen of the Island of the Riches of the World.'

'Then I'll go with you,' Ciad said.

The giant agreed to this, and all sailed off.

They sailed away and away, far further

than I could tell you, and twice as far as you could tell me, until at length they reached the island.

The giant said to Ciad: 'Send your men on the island first, and demand the Riches of the World."

Ciad agreed to this, and sent his men on the island on a morning, but when night fell they had not come back. Next day Ciad himself went in search of them. In the second valley, he found his thirty men lying in blood. He said: 'This is the giant's doing.'

So he went back to his ship and told his two brothers if they would engage the giant's men, he would engage the giant himself. This was agreed to, and they attacked the giant and his men.

A fiercer and bloodier battle was never fought on sea or land. The noise and the din were so loud, and the battling was so fierce, that the seals came down from the North Seas, the whales up from the deeps of the ocean, and the little red fishes, too, from the sea-meadows, gathering around the ship to watch the fight. For the length of a day they battled, and when the sun was one hour above the Western waters, Ceud, Mith-Ceud, and the giant's men were all of them dead, but Ciad and the giant still battled. When the hoop of the sun was on the waters, the giant, finding himself weakening too fast, gave three calls. Ciad saw the blue mist coming down; he gave a bound into the air and drove his spear to the giant's heart, and killed him.

Then he went on the island, and stood his two brothers up against a rock facing the east, with helmets on their heads, and shields and spears in their hands. On the next morning he set out to travel over the island, and at night he came to a little hut, where he found one old hag. He asked her if she had no company.

She said: 'Yes, I have plenty of that.'

He asked to see her company.

She struck her staff on the hearthstone, and up sprang nine other hags as old and as ugly as herself. She struck the staff again

upon the hearthstone, and then they were the nine most beautiful damsels Ciad had ever seen.

The hag said: 'If you stay with me, you can have your choice of these nine beautiful damsels for your wife.'

But Ciad remembered Dark Eye of France, and also remembered his geasa, and he said to the hag, he would have none of them.

Then she struck her staff upon the ground angrily, and they all disappeared.

He asked for supper and a bed for the night, and the old hag gave him the toes and the tongue of a rabbit for supper. She gave him a heather bed that scored and cut him, and an old black cat for a bedfellow.

In the morning he told the hag that he was looking for the queen of this island.

She said: 'I am the queen.'

'If that is so,' he said, 'I demand the bottle of loca and the Riches of the World.'

'That,' she said, 'I am glad you cannot have.'

'If I cannot have it,' he said, 'I will take your staff and break your old bones.'

'It's like a hero to do that,' she said scoffingly; 'but even if you made meal of my old bones, you would not be nearer the bottle of loca and the Riches of the World.'

Ciad asked how that was.

She said: 'Feach-An-Chruic [the Terrible Man of the Hill] took away the bottle of loca and the Riches of the World from me two hundred years ago.'

'I do not believe it,' said Ciad.

But she took him outside and showed him the hoof tracks of the Feach's horses, where last night's rains were still lying in them.

'Where does Feach-An-Chruic live?' Ciad asked.

'He lives a third part of the world from here,' the hag said.

'How may I get there?' Ciad said.

'As best you can,' said the hag.

'By this and by that,' said Ciad, seizing her staff, 'I'll make meal of your old bones if you don't direct me.'

She took him down to the shore, took a black whistle from her pocket and blew on it, when a little red fish appeared on top of the water.

'There,' she said, 'follow that fish, and it will lead you to Feach-An-Chruic.'

Ciad stepped into his ship, hoisted his sails, and went off after the little red fish.

He went away for long, long days and long, long nights, sailing one-third of the whole world, until at length the little fish ran into a wood-bordered bay. Ciad anchored his ship here, and went on shore.

He travelled over the mountains for three days and three nights, and on the fourth day he found Feach-An-Chruic dividing beef among his men.

Ciad walked up to him, and asked for a bit of the beef.

'By my faith, no!' said Feach-An-Chruic. 'But now that you're here I'll save my beef.'

'How is that?' said Ciad.

'Because I'll divide you among my men,' said Feach-An-Chruic.

'You might not,' said Ciad.

So Ciad and the Feach fell to and fought.

The Feach was a wild and terrible fighter surely, but the courageous spirit of Ciad made him a better. The noise and din and fierceness of the fight was so great that the boars came down from the hills, and the deer came up from the valleys, and the birds came from the woods of the world, to watch it; but before night fell Ciad put the Feach down. Then he put his knee on his breast, and asked him where he would find the bottle of loca and the Riches of the World.

Feach-an-Chruic said: 'If that is what you came for and what you fought for, I'm sorry for you. I had the bottle of loca and the Riches of the World only one night when Feach-An-Choille [the Terrible Man of the Wood] took them from me.'

'I do not believe it,' said Ciad.

But the Feach showed him the footprints of Feach-An-Choille, with last night's rains still lying in them.

'And where does Feach-An-Choille live?' said Ciad.

'He lives a third of the world from here,' said Feach-An-Chruic.

'And how may I get there?' Ciad asked.

'You're a brave man,' said Feach-An-Chruic, 'and I would like to see you succeed.'

With the point of his spear he rang three times on his shield, and a wolf-dog came running up. 'Follow that dog,' said Feach-An-Chruic, 'and he will lead you to Feach-An-Choille.'

Ciad set out after the dog, and he travelled away and away, far further than I could tell you, and twice as far as you could tell me, over hill, height, and hollow, mountain, moor, and scrug, lone valley and green glen, for long and for long, until at length and at last he reached the land of Feach-An-Choille. Travelling through it he came upon a hut, and saw Feach-An-Choille himself standing outside. He was leaning against the end of his hut laughing, and every time he laughed oak trees fell.

'Why do you laugh?' said Ciad, when he reached him.

'I'm laughing for the joy of killing you,' said Feach-An-Choille.

'Wouldn't it be better to laugh after?' said Ciad.

Then he raised his spear, and he and the Feach went at the fight. The noise and the din and the fierceness of the fight was such that the boars came down from the hills, and the deer came up from the valleys, and the birds from the woods of the world loaded the tree tops around, to watch. If Feach-An-Chruic was a great fighter, Feach-An-Choille was a far greater, but as great as he was, Ciad's courageous spirit was still greater, and when the sun was behind the trees in the west, Ciad put the Feach down.

'You're a brave man,' said the Feach, when he was down. 'What can I do for you?'

'You can give me the bottle of loca and the Riches of the World,' said Ciad.

'I cannot,' said the Feach. 'I'm sorry. I had the bottle of loca and the Riches of the World only one night, when the King of Persia took them from me. And now,' said the Feach, 'you may as well return home, for you can never get them from the King of Persia.'

'Why cannot I?' said Ciad.

'Because,' he said, 'the King of Persia, when he got the Riches of the World, called together at once the Seven Wizards of the East, and had them lay spells on him, so that no man could ever conquer him.'

'I'm sorry for that,' said Ciad, 'but I'll not return home; I'll travel on to meet my fate.'

Ciad travelled on for a long time. He came to a plain that was covered with dead men, and on one of the dead men he saw a gold boot and a silver boot. He got hold of the gold boot and tried to pull it off, and the man whom he thought was dead struck him with the other boot and tossed him.

'Who are you?' said Ciad.

'I am Swift Sword, son of the King of Spain, one blow of whose

sword has the power of one thousand men for one thousand years, and would blow the sea dry,' he said. 'This is my army that I brought into the Eastern World, and all of them are killed.'

'I am glad to find you,' said Ciad, 'for I am your cousin Ciad, the son of the King of Norway. Come with me.'

Ciad and Swift Sword set out, and travelled on and on until they came to the lake of the Singing Shore, and travelled by it until they reached a small house. As they came up to the house they saw a white pigeon fly from the chimney at every step they took.

Ciad thought this very strange and that he would go in and find out what it meant. Inside he saw a very beautiful young lady sitting by the fire. She had in her hand a wand covered with scales. She was plucking the scales from it, one by one, and flinging them into the fire, and for every scale she flung into the fire a white pigeon got up and flew from the chimney.

'The blessing of Crom on you,' said Ciad. 'I am Ciad, the son of the King of Norway. I am travelling in search of the King of Persia, to get from him the bottle of loca and the Riches of the World. I should like to know the name of the beautiful damsel I am addressing.'

She said, 'I am Pearl Mouth, daughter of the King of Persia, and am living here all alone, very far from my country and my people.'

'How is that?' said Ciad.

She said: 'A year ago I married Blue Gold, the son of the King of Africa, and on my marriage day he was carried away by force by Mountain of Fierceness, son of the King of Greece, and turned into a pigeon in the Eastern Skies. I have sat here for a year sending off these messengers to find him, but not one of them has come back.'

'I am very sorry for you,' said Ciad.

'And I am very sorry for you,' said Pearl Mouth.

'How is that?' said Ciad.

'Because my father, the King of Persia,' she said, 'cannot be conquered by living man; so you can never force from him the bottle of loca and the Riches of the World.'

'Then I'll die in trying,' said Ciad.

'Isn't it better to get them and live?' Pearl Mouth said.

'But I cannot do that,' Ciad said.

'If you are a very great hero there is just a chance for you,' said Pearl Mouth.

Ciad asked her what that chance was, and she told him that if he would find Mountain of Fierceness, the son of the King of Greece, and conquer him and bring back to her Blue Gold, she would get for him from her father what he wanted.

'Then,' he said, 'I will do that.'

'Not so easily,' said Pearl Mouth, 'for no one in the world can overcome Mountain of Fierceness unless he has the *buaidh* (power of victory) of Soul of Steel, Prince of India.'

'Then,' said Ciad, 'I will set off and find that.'

Away he started, and did not stop until he reached India. He demanded *buaidh* from Soul of Steel.

'That I will not give you,' said Soul of Steel.

Then Ciad said, 'I will fight you for it.'

'You will only throw away your life,' said Soul of Steel, 'for no man can conquer me but one.'

'And who is that one?' said Ciad.

'The man who can kill the Giant of the Great Seas,' said Soul of Steel.

'Then,' said Ciad, 'I'm that man;' and he told his story to Soul of Steel.

Soul of Steel said he was a great hero, surely, and that he was glad to give him *buaidh*.

'Break a branch,' he said, 'from that oak tree that grows before my castle, and it will give you *buaidh*.'

Ciad went to the oak tree and broke a branch, but when it fell to the ground, it sprang up into a great tree, and with every other branch he broke the same thing happened.

Soul of Steel came out and gave him his cloak. He said, 'Spread this under the branch.'

He broke another branch, which fell on the cloak, and he carried it off, and went in search of Mountain of Fierceness.

He travelled away and away before him, far further than I can tell you, and twice as far as you could tell me, over height, hill, and hollow, mountain, moor and scrug, lone valley and green glen, until at last and at length, he found, in Africa, Mountain of Fierceness with all his men, gathered together on a hilltop. He walked up to them, and asked what was happening.

They said Mountain of Fierceness was being married to the Queen of the Indies. He pushed his way to where the priests were marrying them.

Mountain of Fierceness asked the stranger what he wanted.

Ciad said, 'I have come to conquer you.'

'That, my good man, you can't do,' said Mountain of Fierceness. 'It's better for you to return to your home, for I'm getting married.'

'I'll never return until I've taken your life or made you grant me one request,' said Ciad.

'I'll not give you my life, and I'll not grant you one request,' said Mountain of Fierceness. 'But I'll spit you on the point of my spear if you don't leave this and go whence you came.'

Then Ciad asked him to step out for a fight.

'I don't want to take your life or any man's to-day,' said Mountain of Fierceness, 'as I am to be married. Yet no man can overcome me unless he has *buaidh* from Soul of Steel, the Prince of India.'

'And that I have,' said Ciad, throwing the oak branch at his feet.

Mountain of Fierceness looked at this, and then said: 'Will you spare my life?'

'On one condition,' said Ciad, 'and that is that you tell me where Blue Gold, Prince of Africa, whom you carried off from his wife a year ago, is, and how I may get him.'

'Where he is and what he is, I can tell you,' said Mountain of Fierceness, 'and how you may get him, but I very much doubt if ever you can get him. He is a wild pigeon in the Eastern Skies — nothing can catch him but the magic net of the King of Ireland's Druid, and this net could only be purchased by one-third of the Riches of the World; and nothing can disenchant him but nine grains of wheat that lie at the bottom of the Well of the World's End, which can only be emptied by three thousand men in three thousand years.'

When Ciad heard this he bade him good-by. He sent Swift Sword to Ireland to get the loan of the magic net of the King of Ireland's Druid, on the promise of paying him one-third of the Riches of the World, and told Swift Sword to meet him at the Well of the World's End.

Away and away then he travelled, far further than I can tell you, and twice as far as you can tell me. Over hills a hundred miles high, and valleys a hundred miles deep; across plains where living man had never been before, and through great woods that were so far from the world that the birds themselves had never reached them, until at length and at last he reached the Well of the World's End and there he found Swift Sword before him, with the net of the King of Ireland's Druid.

With three blows of the sword Swift Sword blew the Well of the World's End dry, and they took from the bottom the nine grains of wheat. They spread the net in the Eastern World and caught in it a hundred thousand pigeons, amongst them one great wild pigeon, which was Blue Gold.

They gave him to eat the nine grains of wheat, and there stood up a handsome prince before them — Blue Gold.

With him they travelled back away and away, until they came to the Lake of the Singing Shore, and to the little house where they found Pearl Mouth, who was rejoiced to get her Blue Gold back again.

Then the four of them set out, and travelled away and away, over mountains and valleys and great long plains, until they came to her father, the King of Persia, from whom she demanded the bottle of loca and the Riches of the World to give them to Ciad and repay him for his services.

The King of Persia said: 'No man could ever take these from me, but I give them willingly to the brave champion, Ciad.'

He and Swift Sword spent that night in the King of Persia's castle, and in the morning set out for home. When they came to the Plain of Blood, they shook one drop from the bottle of loca on Swift Sword's army, and all of them stood up alive and well.

Ciad then parted with Swift Sword, who was going on to conquer the East, and he himself — for his time was now getting short — did not turn aside, but went direct for home. And on the evening of the day on which the three years and a day would have expired, Ciad stood upon the spot on the seashore from which he had set out, and there he found Dark Eye awaiting him.

He gave her the bottle of loca, and her step-mother's spells were at once taken off her. They went to the island on which he had left his two brothers, Ceud and Mith-Ceud; he shook on them one drop from the bottle of loca, and the two were again alive and well. All of them set out, and sailed to Ciad's father's castle — he and his two brothers and Dark Eye, with the bottle of loca and the Riches of the World.

A messenger was sent at once to France, to invite the King to come to his daughter's marriage, and to bring his sons and his great lords with him. And another messenger brought to the King of Ireland's Druid his magic net and a third of the Riches of the World, and invited the King of Ireland and all his court to come to the marriage also. One hundred kings sat down to the wedding feast. The wedding lasted ninety-nine days and ninety-nine nights, and the last night was better than the first.

Ciad and Dark Eye lived a long life and a happy one, and may you and I do the same.

(from *Donegal Fairy Stories*)

Flory Cantillon's Funeral

by THOMAS CROFTON CROKER

The Cantillon family graveyard was on an island in Ballyheigh Bay in County Kerry. This island was not far from the shore, and a very long time ago was once overflowed by the Atlantic Ocean. The fishermen say they have often seen the ruined walls of an old chapel beneath them in the water, as they sailed over the clear green sea of a sunny afternoon. However this may be, it is well known that the Cantillons were, like most other Irish families, strongly attached to their ancient burial-place; and this attachment led to the custom, when any of the family died, of carrying the corpse to the sea-side, where the coffin was left on the shore within reach of the tide. In the morning it had disappeared, being, as was traditionally believed, conveyed away by the ancestors of the deceased to their family tomb.

Connor Crowe, a County Clare man, was related to the Cantillons by marriage.

'Connor Mac in Cruagh, of the seven quarters of Breintragh,' as he was commonly called, and a proud man he was of the name. Connor, be it known, would drink a quart of salt water, for its medicinal virtues, before breakfast; and for the same reason, I suppose, double that quantity of raw whiskey between breakfast and night, which last he did with as little inconvenience to himself as any man in the barony of Moyferta; and were I to add Clanderalaw and Ibrickan, I don't think I should say wrong.

On the death of Florence Cantillon, Connor Crowe was determined to satisfy himself about the truth of this story of the old church under the sea: so when he heard the news of the old fellow's death, away with him to Ardfert, where Flory was laid out in high style, and a beautiful corpse he made.

Flory had been as jolly and as rollicking a boy in his day as ever was stretched, and his wake was in every respect worthy of him. There was all kind of entertainment and all sort of diversion at it, and no less than three girls got husbands there — more luck to them. Everything was as it should be; all that side of the country, from Dingle to Tarbert, was at the funeral. The keen was sung long and bitterly; and according to the family custom, the coffin was carried to Ballyheigh strand, where it was laid upon the shore

with a prayer for the repose of the dead.

The mourners departed, one group after another, and at last Connor Crowe was left alone: he then pulled out his whiskey bottle, his drop of comfort, as he called it, which he required, being in grief; and down he sat upon a big stone that was sheltered by a projecting rock, and partly concealed from view, to await with patience the appearance of the ghostly undertakers.

The evening came on mild and beautiful; he whistled an old air which he had heard in his childhood, hoping to keep idle fears out of his head: but the wild strain of that melody brought a thousand recollections with it, which only made the twilight appear more pensive.

'If 'twas near the gloomy tower of Dunmore, in my own sweet country, I was,' said Connor Crowe, with a sigh, 'one might well believe that the prisoners, who were murdered long ago there in the vaults under the castle, would be the hands to carry off the coffin out of envy, for never a one of them was buried decently, nor had as much as a coffin amongst them all. 'Tis often, sure enough, I have heard lamentations and great mourning coming from the vaults of Dunmore Castle; but,' continued he, after fondly pressing his lips to the mouth of his companion and silent comforter, the whiskey bottle, 'didn't I know all the time well enough, 'twas the dismal sounding waves working through the cliffs and hollows of the rocks, and fretting themselves to foam. Oh, then, Dunmore Castle, it is you that are the gloomy-looking tower on a gloomy day, with the gloomy hills behind you; when one has gloomy thoughts on their heart, and sees you like a ghost rising out of the smoke made by the kelp burners on the strand, there is, the Lord save us! as fearful a look about you as about the Blue Man's Lake at midnight. Well then, any how,' said Connor, after a pause, 'is it not a blessed night, though surely the moon looks mighty pale in the face? St. Senan himself between us and all kinds of harm.'

It was, in truth, a lovely moonlight night; nothing was to be seen around but the dark rocks, and the white pebbly beach, upon which the sea broke with a hoarse and melancholy murmur. Connor, notwithstanding his frequent draughts, felt rather queerish, and almost began to repent his curiosity. It was certainly a solemn sight to behold the black coffin resting upon the white strand. His imagination gradually converted the deep moaning of old ocean into a mournful wail for the dead, and from the shadowy recesses of the rocks he imaged forth strange and visionary forms.

As the night advanced Connor became weary with watching; he caught himself more than once in the fact of nodding, when suddenly giving his head a shake, he would look towards the black coffin. But the narrow house of death remained unmoved before him.

It was long past midnight, and the moon was sinking into the

sea, when he heard the sound of many voices, which gradually became stronger, above the heavy and monotonous roll of the sea: he listened, and presently could distinguish a keen, of exquisite sweetness, the notes of which rose and fell with the heaving of the waves, whose deep murmur mingled with and supported the strain!

The keen grew louder and louder, and seemed to approach the beach, and then fell into a low plaintive wail. As it ended Connor beheld a number of strange and, in the dim light, mysterious-looking figures, emerge from the sea, and surround the coffin, which they prepared to launch into the water.

'This comes of marrying with the creatures of earth,' said one of the figures, in a clear, yet hollow tone.

'True,' replied another, with a voice still more fearful, 'our king would never have commanded his gnawing white-toothed waves to devour the rocky roots of the island cemetery, had not his daughter, Durfulla, been buried there by her mortal husband!'

'But the time will come,' said a third, bending over the coffin,

'When mortal eye — our work shall spy,
And mortal ear — our dirge shall hear.'

'Then,' said a fourth, 'our burial of the Cantillons is at an end for ever!'

As this was spoken the coffin was borne from the beach by a retiring wave, and the company of sea people prepared to follow it; but at the moment one chanced to discover Connor Crowe, as fixed with wonder and as motionless with fear as the stone on which he sat.

'The time is come,' cried the unearthly being, 'the time is come; a human eye looks on the forms of ocean, a human ear has heard their voices; farewell to the Cantillons; the sons of the sea are no longer doomed to bury the dust of the earth!'

One after the other turned slowly round, and regarded Connor

Crowe, who still remained as if bound by a spell. Again arose their funeral song; and on the next wave they followed the coffin. The sound of the lamentation died away, and at length nothing was heard but the rush of waters. The coffin and the train of sea people sank over the old churchyard, and never since the funeral of old Flory Cantillon have any of the family been carried to the strand of Ballyheigh, for conveyance to their rightful burial-place, beneath the waves of the Atlantic.

(from *Fairy Legends and Traditions of the South of Ireland*)

Cliona's Wave

by SINÉAD DE VALERA

LOUD noise, as from the surging of a wave, is occasionally heard in the harbour of Glandore, County Cork, both in calm and stormy weather. It is the forerunner of the shifting of the wind to the northwest. It is called the 'Tonn Cliona' or Cliona's Wave and was supposed to portend the death of some great personage.

King Turlough and his Queen Sive had their palace near Glandore, in County Cork. They were married many years and had no children. At last a beautiful baby girl was born. She was called Ethna and was the joy and pride of her parent's hearts.

One lovely day the king and queen were seated at a window in the palace, looking at the beautiful scene that lay before them.

Cloudless sky and sparkling sea,
Cliff and shore and forest tree,
Glen and stream and mountain blue,
Burst at once upon the view.

'Who would not be happy,' said Turlough, 'while looking on such a scene?'

'Well, you and I are certainly very happy,' the queen replied, 'and it is a joy to think that little Ethna is heiress to all this beauty. There she is, sleeping peacefully in her cradle under the hawthorn tree, with her faithful nurse by her side.'

'Sometimes,' said the king, 'I wonder if the nurse is so faithful.

It has been whispered to me that she cares more about Fergus, the gardener, than she does about our little Ethna.'

'Oh, don't mind those idle rumours,' the queen said. 'I am sure she is very attentive to the child. Let us walk down to the sea. It is a pity to be indoors on such a day.'

'Look how calm the water is,' said the king. 'It is almost without a ripple, except where the wavelets break on the beach.'

'Yes, but there is a swell on the sea and the wind is turning to the northeast.'

Suddenly, a loud noise was heard, a noise as from the surging of a wave. Both Turlough and Sive trembled and turned pale.

'That is Cliona's Wave!' cried the king in great alarm.

'Yes,' said the queen, 'the wave that gives warning that some terrible sorrow is to come to us. Can we do nothing to lessen the fairy's power?'

'Alas, no! No one is strong enough to lessen the power of the fairy, Cliona.'

They returned in haste to the palace. Everything there showed signs of trouble and confusion.

'Oh, what has happened?' cried the queen.

There was silence for a moment and then Turlough and Sive were told that their dear child was lost. The nurse had left the baby sleeping under the hawthorn tree and had gone some distance away to speak to the gardener. When she returned the child was gone. She had been stolen by the fairies.

'I knew,' said Turlough, 'that some great sorrow was coming to us when we heard the sound of Cliona's Wave.'

'Oh, why,' asked Sive, turning to the nurse, 'did you leave our child alone?'

'It is just as if she had died,' said the king, 'for we shall never see her again."

From that time happiness and peace were gone from the palace. Sorrow and gloom reigned in their stead. Years went by without bringing any tidings of Ethna. Turlough and Sive tried to rule wisely and to look after the welfare of their subjects, but they never ceased to pine for the child they had lost.

One day Sive was walking along a road just outside the palace when she saw a woman and a little boy coming towards her. As the woman drew nearer, the queen saw that she looked very

tired and ill. In a moment she had fallen to the ground. One of the queen's waiting women hurried into the palace to call for help. When the woman was brought in, it was found that she was dying. She whispered to the queen: 'My husband, who was a chieftain in a territory some miles east from here, was killed when defending his home from his enemies. I travelled here to ask you to befriend my little Donal when I am gone."

In a few moments the woman was dead.

The queen felt it was her duty to take care of the little boy. Gradually she came to love him as if he were her own child. She and the king determined to make him their heir. They often spoke to him of Ethna and it became the great wish of his heart to bring her back to her home.

Years passed and Donal grew to be a fine, handsome youth. He was as good as he was handsome. He had a great love of the sea and used to go many miles from land in a boat which the queen had given him. Sometimes he would take provisions with him and would spend hours on the water.

One warm August day when the sea was like a beautiful spreading lake under a blue sky, Donal ventured farther and farther from the shore. As he went southward, he saw in the distance a small island. It seemed to be covered with emeralds and rubies. As he drew nearer, he saw that rows of rowan trees grew round the coast. Their foliage and berries were what he had thought were gems glistening in the sunshine.

A little cove faced him as he approached the land. He made fast his boat and went in on the island. From the trees came the sound of human voices and, to his amazement, he found that these voices belonged to birds perched on the trees. Numbers of birds were there, brown, black, green and other colours, all chattering away in human speech.

While Donal was wondering at what he saw and heard, he

noticed a strange-looking house in the centre of the island. It was built of stone and had a long, sloping roof.

The birds continued to talk. Donal lay down on the sward near the house and listened to them.

'Yesterday,' said the pigeon, 'I flew to Glandore Castle and rested in the hawthorn tree in the garden. The king and queen were sitting under the tree. They were speaking sadly of the Princess Ethna who was carried away to fairyland many years ago.'

'They will never see the same Ethna again,' said the raven in a harsh, croaking voice. 'The fairy Cliona holds her a captive in her court.'

'Oh, you always have the worst news!' exclaimed the thrush.

'Well, I know what I am talking about,' retorted the raven.

'Peace, peace,' said the gentle voice of the dove.

'Yes,' said the little wren, 'let us be bright and cheerful.'

'Was Ethna the name of the princess?' asked the swallow from her nest under the roof of the house.

'Yes,' replied the pigeon, 'Ethna was her name.'

'Well, then I know where she is. In the spring, when we swallows were coming back to Ireland, we flew over a fairy fort some miles north of Glandore. I stopped to take a sip of water from a river near by. I saw a mortal maiden in the fort and heard the fairies call her Ethna.'

Just then Donal saw a boat approaching the island. An old, bent man came on shore.

'You are the first visitor that has come to my island home,' he said to Donal, 'and I bid you welcome.'

Donal thanked him and told him he had been much interested in listening to the conversation of the birds.

'Yes,' said the old man, 'these birds see and hear a great deal in their flights from the island and, as they have the gift of speech, they tell me everything that happens.'

'I have heard very important news from them,' said Donal.

'What is that news?'

'It is about the Princess Ethna, who was years ago taken from her father's home by the fairies. The birds say she is in Cliona's fort.'

The old man shook his head.

'Cliona has wonderful magic powers and, even if you could reach the fort, it would be difficult to rescue the princess. I can help you, however, if you are brave enough to attempt to bring Ethna back.'

'I would do anything to restore her to her parents.'

'Well, then I will give you all the help I can but there will be difficulties and hardships in your way. Cliona's fort is several miles north from Glandore. I will send the pigeon to be your guide by day and the owl to lead you at night.'

'But how will I know the place?' asked Donal.

'You will come to a great rock in the middle of a circular space. Round this rock is a row of smaller stones. This place is Carrig Cliona, that is Cliona's rock. It is useless to approach the fort by day. Wait for a moonlight night!'

'The moon is full at present and I should like to reach the fort tomorrow night.'

'You can do that if you return home now and set out in the morning.'

'I will take the fastest horse in the stable,' said Donal.

'No,' said the man, 'You must go on foot. When you have travelled about twenty miles, you will come to a little house half-hidden by trees. I will send one of my birds to tell the woman of the house to expect you.'

'But how shall I succeed in freeing Ethna from the fairy's spell?'

'That will not be easy. Cliona is very clever. She can take the form of different animals. She can become a deer, a hound or a rabbit but whatever shape she assumes, her green eyes remain the same. Before you set out on your journey tomorrow, cut a branch of the hawthorn tree in the palace garden, a branch with berries on it. If you can manage to strike Cliona with the branch, you will have her in your power and she must do as you wish.'

'And how shall I find Ethna?'

'Command Cliona to call her forth and the princess will gladly come. Do not on any account enter the fort yourself. You must not eat, drink nor speak from the time you leave the island till you reach the house among the trees. Now take my blessing and hasten away.'

As Donal sailed from the shore, the birds sang in a chorus:

> 'Happy will the princess be,
> When young Donal sets her free,
> He will break the cruel spell,
> And the fairy's power will quell.
> May kind fortune on him smile,
> As he leaves our wooded isle.'

Everyone in the palace had retired to rest before Donal

returned. The night was warm and he slept in a summer house in the garden. Early in the morning he went to the hawthorn tree to cut the berried branch. There, sitting on the top of the tree was the pigeon which was to be his guide.

As Donal travelled on, the day became very hot and he felt tired, hungry and thirsty. He saw a woman coming toward him. She had a basket full of delicious fruit in one hand and a glass of mead in the other. She offered him the fruit and mead. Donal longed to take them but he remembered he must not speak, eat nor drink. He gave one longing look at the good things, shook his head and passed on.

When he had gone a little distance he looked back to the place where he had met the woman but she was nowhere to be seen, though that part of the road was quite straight, without bend or turning. The pigeon acted as his guide till

he reached the house among the trees. Then the bird turned and flew southward. To his great surprise, he saw, standing at the door of the house, the woman who had offered him the food and drink.

'You are heartily welcome,' she said.

Donal thanked her and followed her into the house.

'You have bravely borne hunger, thirst and weariness,' said the woman, 'and now you will have your reward.'

She led Donal into the room where a delicious meal was prepared for him. When he had finished his meal she told him to go into the inner room.

'There is a bed,' she said, 'where you can rest till you hear the owl's cry.'

Donal was glad to rest and soon he fell into a deep sleep. He was awakened by the hooting of the owl. He went to the window and by the light of the moon saw the bird on the branch of a tree. As he was leaving the house, the woman said to him:

'If you succeed in your effort to free the princess, there will be food and rest for both of you here on your return journey. Take this horn,' she said, 'and blow it three times when you reach the fairy fort. Cliona will then appear before you.'

Donal again thanked the woman and followed in the direction in which the owl flitted from tree to tree. He came in sight of Cliona's rock. He blew the horn once, twice, three times. Out from the fort walked Cliona. She was very beautiful but there was a cruel gleam in her green eyes.

As she came near to where Donal stood, he attempted to strike her with the hawthorn branch. Immediately, she changed into a white rabbit and ran round and round the court. Then darkness fell. Donal felt something descend on his shoulder. It was the owl whose voice whispered in his ear:

'I will tell you when the rabbit is coming close to where you stand and will warn you when to strike. . . .'

'Now,' said the owl, after a few seconds.

A piercing shriek was heard. The darkness cleared away and

Cliona stood there, weeping and wringing her hands.

'Command the Princess Ethna to come forth,' said Donal.

'Come, Ethna, come,' called Cliona, as she herself disappeared into the fort.

From the centre of the court Ethna approached the surrounding rocks. She stepped outside and looked around her in wonder and joy.

'Oh,' she exclaimed, 'what a beautiful world! But where shall I find the loving friends I have so often seen in my dreams?'

'Come with me,' said Donal, 'and their joy will be greater even than yours when you are all re-united.'

The owl led them back to the little house where the woman gave them a warm welcome. When they were departing on their homeward journey she said to them:

'There will be great rejoicing in the palace when you return and soon there will be a happy wedding there.'

The king and queen wept for joy when they saw their loved child again. Everyone in the palace shared in their delight.

The woman's words came true, for Donal and Ethna were married and lived happily ever after.

(from *The Emerald Ring*)

The Wonderful Tune

by THOMAS CROFTON CROKER

Maurice Connor was the king, and that's no small word, of all the pipers in Munster. He could play jig and planxty without end, and Ollistrum's March, and the Eagle's Whistle, and the Hen's Concert, and odd tunes of every sort and kind. But he knew one far more surprising than the rest, which had in it the power to set everything dead or alive dancing.

In what way he learned it is beyond my knowledge, for he was mighty cautious about telling how he came by so wonderful a tune. At the very first note of that tune the brogues began shaking upon the feet of all who heard it — old or young, it mattered not — just as if their brogues had the ague; then the feet began going, going, going from under them, and at last up and away with them, dancing like mad! whisking here, there, and everywhere, like a straw in a storm — there was no halting while the music lasted!

Not a fair, nor a wedding, nor a patron in the seven parishes round, was counted worth the speaking of without 'blind Maurice and his pipes.' His mother, poor woman, used to lead him about from one place to another just like a dog.

Down through Iveragh — a place that ought to be proud of it-

self, for 'tis Daniel O'Connell's country — Maurice Connor and his mother were taking their rounds. Beyond all other places Iveragh is the place for stormy coasts and steep mountains: as proper a spot it is as any in Ireland to get yourself drowned, or your neck broken on the land, should you prefer that. But, notwithstanding, in Ballinskellig bay there is a neat bit of ground, well fitted for diversion, and down from it, towards the water, is a clean smooth piece of strand, the dead image of a calm summer's sea on a moon-light night, with just the curl of the small waves upon it.

Here it was that Maurice's music had brought from all parts a great gathering of the young men and the young women — *O the darlints!* for 'twas not every day the strand of Trafraska was stirred up by the voice of a bagpipe. The dance began; and as pretty a rinkafadda it was as ever was danced.

'Brave music,' said everybody, 'and well done,' when Maurice stopped.

'More power to your elbow, Maurice, and a fair wind in the bellows,' cried Paddy Dorman, a hump-backed dancing-master, who was there to keep order.

''Tis a pity,' said he, 'if we'd let the piper run dry after such music; 'twould be a disgrace to Iveragh, that didn't come on it since the week of the three Sundays.'

So as well became him, for he was always a decent man, says he, 'Did you drink, piper?'

'I will, sir,' said Maurice, answering the question on the safe side, for you never yet knew piper or school-master who refused his drink.

'What will you drink, Maurice?' says Paddy.

'I'm no ways particular,' says Maurice; 'I drink anything, and give God thanks, barring *raw* water: but if 'tis all the same to you, Mister Dorman, may be you wouldn't lend me the loan of a glass of whiskey.'

'I've no glass, Maurice,' said Paddy; 'I've only the bottle.'

'Let that be no hindrance,' answered Maurice; 'my mouth just holds a glass to the drop; often I've tried it sure.'

So Paddy Dorman trusted him with the bottle — more fool was he; and, to his cost, he found that though Maurice's mouth might not hold more than the glass at one time, yet, owing to the hole in his throat, it took many a filling.

'That was no bad whiskey neither,' says Maurice, handing back the empty bottle.

'By the holy frost, then!' says Paddy, ''tis but *could* comfort there's in that bottle now; and 'tis your word we must take for the strength of the whiskey, for you've left us no sample to judge by;' and to be sure Maurice had not.

Now I need not tell any gentleman or lady with common understanding, that if he or she was to drink an honest bottle of whiskey at one pull, it is not at all the same thing as drinking a bottle of water; and in the whole course of my life I never knew more than five men who could do so without being overtaken by the liquor. Of these Maurice Connor was not one, though he had a stiff head enough of his own — he was fairly tipsy. Don't think I blame him for it; 'tis often a good man's case; but true is the word that says, 'when liquor's in sense is out;' and puff, at a breath, before you could say 'Lord, save us!' out he blasted his wonderful tune.

'Twas really then beyond all belief or telling the dancing. Maurice himself could not keep quiet; staggering now on one leg, now on the other, and rolling about like a ship in a cross sea, trying to humour the tune. There was his mother too, moving her old bones as light as the youngest girl of them all; but her dancing,

no, nor the dancing of all the rest, is not worthy the speaking about
to the work that was going on down upon the strand. Every inch
of it covered with all manner of fish jumping and plunging about
to the music, and every moment more and more would tumble in
out of the water, charmed by the wonderful tune. Crabs of mons-
trous size spun round and round on one claw with the nimbleness
of a dancing-master, and twirled and tossed their other claws about
like limbs that did not belong to them. It was a sight surprising to
behold. But perhaps you may have heard of Father Florence
Conry, a Franciscan friar, and a great Irish poet; *bolg an dana*, as
they used to call him — a wallet of poems. If you have not, he was
as pleasant a man as one would wish to drink with of a hot summer's
day; and he has rhymed out all about the dancing fishes so neatly,
that it would be a thousand pities not to give you his verses; so
here's my hand at an upset of them into English:—

> The big seals in motion
> Like waves of the ocean,
>   Or gouty feet prancing,
> Came heading the gay fish,
> Crabs, lobsters, and cray-fish,
>   Determined on dancing.
>
> The sweet sounds they followed,
> The gasping cod swallow'd;
>   'Twas wonderful, really!
> And turbot and flounder,
> 'Mid fish that were rounder,
>   Just caper'd as gaily.
>
> John-dories came tripping;
> Dull hake by their skipping
>   To frisk it seem'd given;
> Bright mackerel went springing,

Like small rainbows winging
   Their flight up to heaven.

The whiting and haddock
Left salt water paddock
   This dance to be put in:
Where skate with flat faces
Edged out some odd plaices;
   But soles kept their footing.

Sprats and herrings in powers
Of silvery showers
   All number out-number'd.
And great ling so lengthy
Were there in such plenty
   The shore was encumber'd.

The scollop and oyster
Their two shells did roister,
   Like castanets fitting;
While limpets moved clearly,
And rocks very nearly
   With laughter were splitting.

Never was such an 'ullabullo in this world, before or since; 'twas as if heaven and earth were coming together; and all out of Maurice Connor's wonderful tune!

In the height of all these doings, what should there be dancing among the outlandish set of fishes but a beautiful young woman — as beautiful as the dawn of day! She had a cocked hat upon her head: from under it her long green hair — just the colour of the sea — fell down behind, without hindrance to her dancing. Her teeth were like rows of pearl; her lips for all the world looked like red coral; and she had an elegant gown, as white as the foam of the wave, with little rows of purple and red sea-weeds settled out upon it; for you never yet saw a lady, under the water or over the water, who had not a good notion of dressing herself out.

Up she danced at last to Maurice, who was flinging his feet from under him as fast as hops — for nothing in this world could keep still while that tune of his was going on — and says she to him, chanting it out with a voice as sweet as honey —

'I'm a lady of honour
  Who lives in the sea:
Come down, Maurice Connor,
  And be married to me.
Silver plates and gold dishes
  You shall have, and shall be
The king of the fishes,
  When you're married to me.'

Drink was strong in Maurice's head, and out he chanted in return for her great civility. It is not every lady, may be, that would be after making such an offer to a blind piper; 'twas only right in him to give her as good as she gave herself — so says Maurice —

'I'm obliged to you, madam:
  Off a gold dish or plate,
If a king, and I had 'em,
  I could dine in great state.
With your own father's daughter
  I'd be sure to agree;
But to drink the salt water
  Wouldn't do so with me!'

112

The lady looked at him quite amazed, and swinging her head from side to side like a great scholar, 'Well,' says she, 'Maurice, if you're not a poet, where is poetry to be found?'

In this way they kept on at it, framing high compliments; one answering the other, and their feet going with the music as fast as their tongues. All the fish kept dancing too; Maurice heard the clatter and was afraid to stop playing lest it might be displeasing to the fish, and not knowing what so many of them may take it into their heads to do to him if they got vexed.

Well, the lady with the green hair kept on coaxing of Maurice with soft speeches, till at last she overpersuaded him to promise to marry her, and be king over the fishes, great and small. Maurice was well fitted to be their king, if they wanted one that could make them dance; and he surely would drink, barring the salt water, with any fish of them all.

When Maurice's mother saw him, with that unnatural thing in the form of a green-haired lady as his guide, and he and she dancing down together so lovingly to the water's edge, through the thick of the fishes, she called out after him to stop and come back.

'Oh then,' says she, 'as if I was not widow enough before, there he is going away from me to be married to that scaly woman. And who knows but 'tis grandmother I may be to a hake or a cod — Lord help and pity me, but 'tis a mighty unnatural thing! and may be 'tis boiling and eating my own grandchild I'll be, with a bit of salt butter, and I not knowing it! Oh, Maurice, Maurice, if there's any love or nature left in you, come back to your own *ould* mother, who reared you like a decent Christian!' Then the poor woman began to cry and ullagoane so finely that it would do any one good to hear her.

Maurice was not long getting to the rim of the water; there he kept playing and dancing on as if nothing was the matter, and a great thundering wave coming in towards him ready to swallow him up alive; but as he could not see it, he did not fear it. His mother it was who saw it plainly through the big tears that were rolling down her cheeks; and though she saw it, and her heart was aching as much as ever mother's heart ached for a son, she kept dancing, dancing all the time for the bare life of her. Certain it was she could not help it, for Maurice never stopped playing that wonderful tune of his.

He only turned the bothered ear to the sound of his mother's voice, fearing it might put him out in his steps, and all the answer he made back was, 'Whisht with you, mother — sure I'm going to be king over the fishes down in the sea, and for a token of luck, and a sign that I'm alive and well, I'll send you in, every twelve-month on this day, a piece of burned wood to Trafraska.' Maurice had not the power to say a word more, for the strange lady with the green hair, seeing the wave just upon them, covered him up with herself in a thing like a cloak with a big hood to it, and the wave curling over twice as high as their heads, burst upon the strand, with a rush and a roar that might be heard as far as Cape Clear.

That day twelvemonth the piece of burned wood came ashore in Trafraska. It was a queer thing for Maurice to think of sending all the way from the bottom of the sea. A gown or a pair of shoes would have been something like a present for his poor mother; but he had said it, and he kept his word. The bit of burned wood regularly came ashore on the appointed day for as good, ay, and better than a hundred years. The day is now forgotten, and may be that is the reason why people say how Maurice Connor has stopped sending the luck-token to his mother. Poor woman, she did not live to get as much as one of them; for what through the loss of Maurice, and the fear of eating her own grandchildren, she died in three weeks after the dance. Some say it was the fatigue that killed her, but whichever it was, Mrs. Connor was decently buried with her own people.

Seafaring people have often heard, off the coast of Kerry, on a still night, the sound of music coming up from the water; and some, who have had good ears, could plainly distinguish Maurice Connor's voice singing these words to his pipes —

'Beautiful shore, with thy spreading strand,
Thy crystal water, and diamond sand;
Never would I have parted from thee,
But for the sake of my fair ladie.'

(from *Fairy Legends and Traditions of the South of Ireland*)

The Fisherman's Son and the Gruagach

by JEREMIAH CURTIN

There was an old fisherman once in Erin who had a wife and one son.

The old fisherman used to go about with a fishing-rod and tackle to the rivers and lochs and every place where fish resort, and he was killing salmon and other fish to keep the life in himself and his wife and son.

The son was not so keen nor so wise as another, and the father was instructing him every day in fishing, so that if himself should be taken from the world, the son would be able to support the old mother and get his own living.

One day when the father and son were fishing in a river near the sea, they looked out over the water and saw a small dark speck on the waves. It grew larger and larger, till they saw a boat, and when the boat drew near they saw a man sitting in the stern of it.

There was a nice beach near the place where they were fishing. The man brought the boat straight to the beach, and stepping out drew it up on the sand.

They saw then that the stranger was a man of high birth.

After he had put the boat high on the sand, he came to where the two were at work, and said: 'Old fisherman, you'd better let this son of yours with me for a year and a day, and I will make a very wise man of him. I am the Gruagach na g-cleasan (Gruagach of tricks), and I'll bind myself to be here with your son this day year.'

'I can't let him go,' said the old fisherman, ''till he gets his mother's advice.'

'Whatever goes as far as women I'll have nothing to do with,' said the Gruagach. 'You had better give him to me now, and let the mother alone.'

They talked till at last the fisherman promised to let his son go for the year and a day. Then the Gruagach gave his word to have the boy there at the seashore that day year.

The Gruagach and the boy went into the boat and sailed away.

When the year and a day were over, the old fisherman went to the same place where he had parted with his son and the Gruagach, and stood looking over the sea, thinking would he see his son that day.

At last he saw a black spot on the water, then a boat. When it was near he saw two men sitting in the stern of the boat. When it touched land, the two, who were of high birth in appearance, jumped out, and one of them pulled the boat to the top of the strand.

Then that one, followed by the other, came to where the old fisherman was waiting, and asked: 'What trouble is on you now, my good man?'

'I had a son that wasn't so keen nor so wise as another, and myself and this son were here fishing, and a stranger came, like yourself to-day, and asked would I let my son with him for a year and a day. I let the son go, and the man promised to be here with him to-day, and that's why I am waiting at this place now.'

'Well,' said the Gruagach, 'am I your son?'

'You are not,' said the fisherman.

'Is this man here your son?'

'I don't know him,' said the fisherman.

'Well, then, he is all you will have in place of your son,' said the Gruagach.

The old man looked again, and knew his son. He caught hold of him and welcomed him home.

'Now,' said the Gruagach, 'isn't he a better man than he was a year ago?'

'Oh, he's nearly a smart man now!' said the old fisherman.

'Well,' said the Gruagach, 'will you let him with me for another year and a day?'

'I will not,' said the old man; 'I want him myself.'

The Gruagach then begged and craved till the fisherman promised to let the son with him for a year and a day again.

But the old man forgot to take his word of the Gruagach to bring back the son at the end of the time; and when the Gruagach and the boy were in the boat, and had pushed out to sea, the Gruagach shouted to the old man: 'I kept my promise to bring

back your son to-day. I haven't given you my word at all now. I'll not bring him back, and you'll never see him again.'

The fisherman went home with a heavy and sorrowful heart, and the old woman scolded him all that night till next morning for letting her son go with the Gruagach a second time.

Then himself and the old woman were lamenting a quarter of a year; and when another quarter had passed, he said to her: 'I'll leave you here now, and I'll be walking on myself till I wear my legs off up to my knees, and from my knees to my waist, till I find where is my son.'

So away went the old man walking, and he used to spend but one night in a house, and not two nights in any house, till his feet were all in blisters. One evening late he came to a hut where there was an old woman sitting at a fire.

'Poor man!' said she, when she laid eyes on him, 'it's a great distress you are in, to be so disfigured with wounds and sores. What is the trouble that's on you?'

'I had a son,' said the old man, 'and the Gruagach na g-cleasan came on a day and took him from me.'

'Oh, poor man!' said she. 'I have a son with that same Gruagach these twelve years, and I have never been able to get him back or get sight of him, and I'm in dread you'll not be able to get your son either. But to-morrow, in the morning, I'll tell you all I know, and show you the road you must go to find the house of the Gruagach na g-cleasan.'

Next morning she showed the old fisherman the road. He was to come to the place by evening.

When he came and entered the house, the Gruagach shook hands with him, and said: 'You are welcome, old fisherman. It was I that put this journey on you, and made you come here looking for your son.'

'It was no one else but you,' said the fisherman.

'Well,' said the Gruagach, 'you won't see your son to-day. At noon to-morrow I'll put a whistle in my mouth and call together all the birds in my place, and they'll come. Among others will be twelve doves. I'll put my hand in my pocket, this way, and take out wheat and throw it before them on the ground. The doves will eat the wheat, and you must pick your son out of the twelve. If you find him, you'll have him; if you don't, you'll never get him again.'

After the Gruagach had said these words the old man ate his

supper and went to bed.

In the dead of night the old fisherman's son came.

'Oh, father!' said he, 'it would be hard for you to pick me out among the twelve doves, if you had to do it alone; but I'll tell you. When the Gruagach calls us in, and we go to pick up the wheat, I'll make a ring around the others, walking for myself; and as I go I'll give some of them a tip of my bill, and I'll lift my wings when I'm striking them. There was a spot under one of my arms when I left home, and you'll see that spot under my wing when I raise it to-morrow. Don't miss the bird that I'll be, and don't let your eyes off it; if you do, you'll lose me forever.'

Next morning the old man rose, had his breakfast, and kept thinking of what his son had told him.

At midday the Gruagach took his whistle and blew. Birds came to him from every part, and among others the twelve doves.

He took wheat from his pocket, threw it to the doves, and said to the father: 'Now pick out your son from the twelve.'

The old man was watching, and soon he saw one of the doves walking around the other eleven and hitting some of them a clip of its bill, and then it raised its wings, and the old man saw the spot. The bird let its wings down again, and went to eating with the rest.

The father never let his eyes off the bird. After a while he said to the Gruagach: 'I'll have that bird there for my son.'

'Well,' said the Gruagach, 'that is your son. I can't blame you for having him; but I blame your instructor for the information he gave you, and I give him my curse.'

So the old fisherman got his son back in his proper shape, and away they went, father and son, from the house of the Gruagach. The old man felt stronger now, and they never stopped travelling a day till they came home.

The old mother was very glad to see her son, and see him such a wise, smart man.

After coming home they had no means but the fishing; they were as poor as ever before.

At this time it was given out at every crossroad in Erin, and in all public places in the kingdom, that there were to be great horse-races.

Now, when the day came, the old fisherman's son said:

'Come away with me, father, to the races.'

The old man went with him, and when they were near the race-

course, the son said: 'Stop here till I tell you this: I'll make myself into the best horse that's here to-day, and do you take me to the place where the races are to be, and when you take me in, I'll open my mouth, trying to kill and eat every man that'll be near me, I'll have such life and swiftness; and do you find a rider for me that'll ride me, and don't let me go till the other horses are far ahead on the course. Then let me go. I'll come up to them, and I'll run ahead of them and win the race. After that every rich man there will want to buy me of you; but don't you sell me to any man for less than five hundred pounds; and be sure you get that price for me. And when you have the gold, and you are giving me up, take the bit out of my mouth, and don't sell the bridle for any money. Then come to this spot, shake the bridle, and I'll be here in my own form before you.'

The son made himself a horse, and the old fisherman took him to the race. He reared and snorted, trying to take the head off every man that came near him.

The old man shouted for a rider. A rider came; he mounted the horse and held him in. The old man didn't let him start till the other horses were well ahead on the course; then he let him go.

The new horse caught up with the others and shot past them. So they had not gone half way when he was in at the winning-post.

When the race was ended, there was a great noise over the strange horse. Men crowded around the old fisherman from every corner of the field, asking what would he take for the horse.

'Five hundred pounds,' said he.

'Here 'tis for you,' said the next man to him.

In a moment the horse was sold, and the money in the old man's pocket. Then he pulled the bridle off the horse's head, and made his way out of the place as fast as ever he could.

It was not long till he was at the spot where the son had told him what to do. The minute he came, he shook the bridle, and the son was there before him in his own shape and features.

Oh, but the old fisherman was glad when he had his son with him again, and the money in his pocket!

The two went home together. They had money enough now to live, and quit the fishing. They had plenty to eat and drink, and they spent their lives in ease and comfort till the next year, when it was given out at all the cross-roads in Erin, and every public place in the kingdom, that there was to be a great hunting with hounds, in the same place where the races had been the year before.

When the day came, the fisherman's son said: 'Come, father, let us go away to this hunting.'

'Ah!' said the old man, 'what do we want to go for? Haven't we plenty to eat at home, with money enough and to spare? What do we care for hunting with hounds?'

'Oh! they'll give us more money,' said the son, 'if we go.'

The fisherman listened to his son, and away they went.

When the two came to the spot where the son had made a horse of himself the year before, he stopped, and said to the father, 'I'll make a hound of myself to-day, and when you bring me in sight of the game, you'll see me wild with jumping and trying to get away; but do you hold me fast till the right time comes, then let go. I'll sweep ahead of every hound in the field, catch the game, and win the prize for you.

'When the hunt is over, so many men will come to buy me that they'll put you in a maze; but be sure you get three hundred pounds for me, and when you have the money, and are giving me up, don't forget to keep my rope. Come to this place, shake the rope, and I'll be here before you, as I am now. If you don't keep the rope, you'll go home without me.'

The son made a hound of himself, and the old father took him to the hunting-ground.

When the hunt began, the hound was springing and jumping

like mad; but the father held him till the others were far out in the field. Then he let him loose, and away went the son.

Soon he was up with the pack, then in front of the pack, and never stopped till he caught the game and won the prize.

When the hunt was over, and the dogs and game brought in, all the people crowded around the old fisherman, saying: 'What do you want of that hound? Better sell him; he's no good to you.'

They put the old man in a maze, there were so many of them, and they pressed him so hard.

He said at last: 'I'll sell the hound; and three hundred pounds is the price I want for him.'

'Here 'tis for you,' said a stranger, putting the money into his hand.

The old man took the money and gave up the dog, without taking off the rope. He forgot his son's warning.

That minute the Gruagach na g-cleasan called out: 'I'll take the worth of my money out of your son now;' and away he went with the hound.

The old man walked home alone that night, and it is a heavy heart he had in him when he came to the old woman without the son. And the two were lamenting their lot till morning.

Still and all, they were better off than the first time they lost their son, as they had plenty of everything, and could live at their ease.

The Gruagach went away home, and put the fisherman's son in a cave of concealment that he had, bound him hand and foot, and tied hard knots on his neck up to the chin. From above there fell on him drops of poison, and every drop that fell went from the skin to the flesh, from the flesh to the bone, from the bone to the marrow, and he sat there under the poison drops, without meat, drink, or rest.

In the Gruagach's house was a servant-maid, and the fisherman's son had been kind to her the time he was in the place before.

On a day when the Gruagach and his eleven sons were out hunting, the maid was going with a tub of dirty water to throw it into the river that ran by the side of the house. She went through the cave of concealment where the fisherman's son was bound, and he asked of her the wetting of his mouth from the tub.

'Oh! the Gruagach would take the life of me,' said she, 'when he comes home, if I gave you as much as one drop.'

'Well,' said he, 'when I was in this house before, and when I had power in my hands, it's good and kind I was to you; and when I

get out of this confinement I'll do you a turn, if you give me the wetting of my mouth now.'

The maid put the tub near his lips.

'Oh! I can't stoop to drink unless you untie one knot from my throat,' said he.

Then she put the tub down, stooped to him, and loosed one knot from his throat. When she loosed the one knot he made an eel of himself, and dropped into the tub. There he began shaking the water, till he put some of it on the ground, and when he had the place about him wet, he sprang from the tub, and slipped along out under the door. The maid caught him; but could not hold him, he was so slippery. He made his way from the door to the river, which ran near the side of the house.

When the Gruagach na g-cleasan came home in the evening with his eleven sons, they went to take a look at the fisherman's son; but he was not to be seen.

Then the Gruagach called the maid, and taking his sword, said: 'I'll take the head off you if you don't tell me this minute what happened while I was gone.'

'Oh!' said the maid, 'he begged so hard for a drop of dirty water to wet his mouth that I hadn't the heart to refuse, for 'tis good he was to me and kind each time he saw me when he was here in the house before. When the water touched his mouth, he made an eel of himself, spilled water out of the tub, and slipped along over the wet place to the river outside. I caught him to bring him back, but I couldn't hold him; in spite of all I could do, he made away.'

The Gruagach dropped his sword, and went to the water side with his sons.

The sons made eleven eels of themselves, and the Gruagach their father was the twelfth. They went around in the water, searching in every place, and there was not a stone in the river that they passed without looking under and around it for the old fisherman's son.

And when he knew that they were after him, he made himself into a salmon; and when they knew he was a salmon, the sons made eleven otters of themselves, and the Gruagach made himself the twelfth.

When the fisherman's son found that twelve otters were after him, he was weak with hunger, and when they had come near, he made himself a whale. But the eleven brothers and their father

made twelve cannon whales of themselves, for they had all gone out of the river, and were in the sea now.

When they were coming near him, the fisherman's son was weak from pursuit and hunger, so he jumped up out of the water, and made a swallow of himself; but the Gruagach and his sons became twelve hawks, and chased the swallows through the air; and as they whirled round and darted, they pressed him hard, till all of them came near the castle of the king of Erin.

Now the king had made a summer-house for his daughter; and where should she be at this time but sitting on the top of the summer-house.

The old fisherman's son dropped down till he was near her; then fell into her lap in the form of a ring. The daughter of the king of Erin took up the ring, looked at it, and put it on her finger. The ring took her fancy, and she was glad.

When the Gruagach and his sons saw this, they let themselves down at the king's castle, having the form of the finest men that could be seen in the kingdom.

When the king's daughter had the ring on her finger she looked at it and liked it.

Then the ring spoke, and said: 'My life is in your hands now; don't part from the ring, and don't let it go to any man, and you'll give me a long life.'

The Gruagach na g-cleasan and his eleven sons went into the

king's castle and played on every instrument known to man, and they showed every sport that could be shown before a king. This they did for three days and three nights. When that time was over, and they were going away, the king spoke up and asked:

'What is the reward that you would like, and what would be pleasing to you from me?'

'We want neither gold nor silver,' said the Gruagach; 'all the reward we ask of you is the ring that I lost on a time, and which is now on your daugher's finger.'

'If my daughter has the ring that you lost, it shall be given to you,' said the king.

Now the ring spoke to the king's daughter and said: 'Don't part with me for anything till you send your trusted man for three gallons of strong spirits and a gallon of wheat; put the spirits and the wheat together in an open barrel before the fire. When your father says you must give up the ring, do you answer back that you have never left the summer-house, that you have nothing on your hand but what is your own and paid for. Your father will say then that you must part with me, and give me up to the stranger. When he forces you in this way, and you can keep me no longer, then throw me into the fire; and you'll see great sport and strange things.'

The king's daughter sent for the spirits and the wheat, had them mixed together, and put in an open barrel before the fire.

The king called the daughter in, and asked: 'Have you the ring which this stranger lost?'

'I have a ring,' said she, 'but it's my own, and I'll not part with it. I'll not give it to him nor to any man.'

'You must,' said the king, 'for my word is pledged, and you must part with the ring!'

When she heard this, she slipped the ring from her finger and threw it into the fire.

That moment the eleven brothers made eleven pairs of tongs of themselves; their father, the old Gruagach, was the twelfth pair.

The twelve jumped into the fire to know in what spark of it would they find the old fisherman's son; and they were a long time working and searching through the fire, when out flew a spark, and into the barrel.

The twelve made themselves men, turned over the barrel, and spilled the wheat on the floor. Then in a twinkling they were twelve cocks strutting around.

They fell to and picked away at the wheat to know which one would find the fisherman's son. Soon one dropped on one side, and a second on the opposite side, until all twelve were lying drunk from the wheat.

Then the old fisherman's son made a fox of himself, and the first cock he came to was the old Gruagach na g-cleasan himself. He took the head off the Gruagach with one bite, and the heads off the eleven brothers with eleven other bites.

When the twelve were dead, the old fisherman's son made himself the finest-looking man in Erin, and began to give music and sport to the king; and he entertained him five times better than had the Gruagach and his eleven sons.

Then the king's daughter fell in love with him, and she set her mind on him to that degree that there was no life for her without him.

When the king saw the straits that his daughter was in, he ordered the marriage without delay.

The wedding lasted for nine days and nine nights, and the ninth night was the best of all.

When the wedding was over, the king felt he was losing his strength, so he took the crown off his own head, and put it on the head of the old fisherman's son, and made him king of Erin in place of himself.

The young couple were the luck, and we the stepping-stones. The presents we got at the marriage were stockings of buttermilk and shoes of paper, and these were worn to the soles of our feet when we got home from the wedding.

(from *Myths and Folk Lore of Ireland*)

The

Sea Maiden

by JOSEPH JACOBS

There was once a poor old fisherman, and one year he was not getting much fish.

On a day of days, while he was fishing, there rose a sea-maiden at the side of his boat, and she asked him, 'Are you getting much fish?'

The old man answered and said, 'Not I.'

'What reward would you give me for sending plenty of fish to you?'

'Ach!' said the old man, 'I have not much to spare.'

'Will you give me the first son you have?' said she.

'I would give ye that, were I to have a son,' said he.

'Then go home, and remember me when your son is twenty years of age, and you yourself will get plenty of fish after this.'

Everything happened as the sea-maiden said, and he himself got plenty of fish; but when the end of the twenty years was nearing, the old man was growing more and more sorrowful and heavy hearted, while he counted each day as it came.

He had rest neither day nor night.

The son asked his father one day, 'Is any one troubling you?'

The old man said, 'Some one is, but that's nought to do with you nor any one else.'

The lad said, 'I *must* know what it is.' His father told him at last how the matter was with him and the sea-maiden.

'Let not that put you in any trouble,' said the son; 'I will not oppose you.'

'You shall not; you shall not go, my son, though I never get fish any more.'

'If you will not let me go with you, go to the smithy, and let the smith make me a great strong sword, and I will go seek my fortune.'

His father went to the smithy, and the smith made a doughty

sword for him. His father came home with the sword. The lad
grasped it and gave it a shake or two, and it flew into a hundred
splinters. He asked his father to go to the smithy and get him another sword in which there should be twice as much weight; and
so his father did, and so likewise it happened to the next sword —
it broke in two halves. Back went the old man to the smithy; and
the smith made a great sword, its like he never made before.

'There's thy sword for thee,' said the smith, 'and the fist must
be good that plays this blade.' The old man gave the sword to his
son; he gave it a shake or two.

'This will do,' said he; 'it's high time now to travel on my way.'

On the next morning he put a saddle on a black horse that his
father had, and he took the world for his pillow. When he went on

a bit, he fell in with the carcass of a sheep beside the road. And there were a great black dog, a falcon, and an otter, and they were quarrelling over the spoil. So they asked him to divide it for them. He came down off the horse, and he divided the carcass amongst the three. Three shares to the dog, two shares to the otter, and a share to the falcon.

'For this,' said the dog, 'if swiftness of foot or sharpness of tooth will give thee aid, mind me, and I will be at thy side.'

Said the otter, 'If the swimming of foot on the ground of a pool will loose thee, mind me, and I will be at thy side.'

Said the falcon, 'If hardship comes on thee, where swiftness of wing or crook of a claw will do good, mind me, and I will be at thy side.'

On this he went onward till he reached a king's house, and he took service to be a herd, and his wages were to be according to the milk of the cattle. He went away with the cattle, and the grazing was but bare. In the evening when he took them home they had not much milk, the place was so bare, and his meat and drink was but spare that night.

On the next day he went on further with them; and at last he came to a place exceedingly grassy, in a green glen, of which he never saw the like.

But about the time when he should drive the cattle homewards, who should he see coming but a great giant with his sword in his hand?

'Hi! Ho!! Hogarach!!!' says the giant. 'Those cattle are mine; they are on my land, and a dead man art thou.'

'I say not that,' says the herd; 'there is no knowing, but that may be easier to say than to do.'

He drew the great clean-sweeping sword, and he neared the giant. The herd drew back his sword, and the head was off the giant in a twinkling. He leaped on the black horse, and he went to look for the giant's house. In went the herd, and that's the place where there was money in plenty, and dresses of each kind in the wardrobe with gold and silver, and each thing finer than the other. At the mouth of night he took himself to the king's house, but he took not a thing from the giant's house. And when the cattle were milked this night there *was* milk. He got good feeding this night, meat and drink without stint, and the king was hugely pleased that he had caught such a herd. He went on for a time in this way, but at last the glen grew bare of grass, and the grazing

was not so good.

So he thought he would go a little further forward in on the giant's land; and he sees a great park of grass. He returned for the cattle, and he put them into the park.

They were but a short time grazing in the park when a great wild giant came full of rage and madness.

'Hi! Haw!! Hogaraich!!!' said the giant. 'It is a drink of thy blood that will quench my thirst this night.'

'There is no knowing,' said the herd, 'but that's easier to say than to do.' And at each other went the men. *There* was shaking of blades! At length and at last it seemed as if the giant would get the victory over the herd. Then he called on the dog, and with one spring the black dog caught the giant by the neck, and swiftly the herd struck off his head.

He went home very tired this night, but it's a wonder if the king's cattle had not milk. The whole family was delighted that they had got such a herd.

Next day he betakes himself to the castle. When he reached the door, a little flattering carlin met him standing in the door.

'All hail and good luck to thee, fisher's son; 'tis I myself am pleased to see thee; great is the honour for this kingdom, for thy like to be come into it — thy coming in is fame for this little bothy; go in first; honour to the gentles; go on, and take breath.'

'In before me, thou crone; I like not flattery out of doors; go in and let's hear thy speech.' In went the crone, and when her back was to him he drew his sword and whips her head off; but the sword flew out of his hand. And swift the crone gripped her head with both hands, and puts it on her neck as it was before. The dog sprung on the crone, and she struck the generous dog with the club of magic; and there he lay. But the herd struggled for a hold of the club of magic, and with one blow on the top of the head she was on earth in the twinkling of an eye. He went forward, up a little, and there was spoil! Gold and silver, and each thing more precious than another, in the crone's castle. He went back to the king's house, and then there was rejoicing.

He followed herding in this way for a time; but one night after he came home, instead of getting 'All hail' and 'Good luck' from the dairymaid, all were at crying and woe.

He asked what cause of woe there was that night.

The dairymaid said, 'There is a great beast with three heads in the loch, and it must get some one every year, and the lot had come this year on the king's daughter, and at midday to-morrow she is to meet the Laidly Beast at the upper end of the loch, but there is a great suitor yonder who is going to rescue her.'

'What suitor is that?' said the herd.

'Oh, he is a great general of arms,' said the dairymaid, 'and when he kills the beast, he will marry the king's daughter, for the king has said that he who could save his daughter should get her to marry.'

But on the morrow, when the time grew near, the king's daughter and this hero of arms went to give a meeting to the beast, and they reached the black rock, at the upper end of the loch. They were but a short time there when the beast stirred in the midst of the loch; but when the general saw this terror of a beast with three heads, he took fright, and he slunk away, and he hid himself. And the king's daughter was under fear and under trembling, with no one at all to save her. Suddenly she sees a doughty handsome youth, riding a black horse, and coming where she was. He was marvellously arrayed and full armed, and his black dog moved after him. 'There is gloom on your face, girl,' said the youth 'what do you here?'

'Oh! that's no matter,' said the king's daughter. 'It's not long I'll be here, at all events.'

'I say not that,' said he.

'A champion fled as likely as you, and not long since,' said she.

'He is a champion who stands the war,' said the youth. And to meet the beast he went with his sword and his dog. But there was a spluttering and splashing between himself and the beast! The dog kept doing all he might, and the king's daughter was palsied by fear of the noise of the beast! One of them would now be under, and now above. But at last he cut one of the heads  off it. It gave one roar, and the son of earth, echo of the rocks, called to its screech, and it drove the loch in spindrift from end to end, and in a twinkling it went out of sight.

'Good luck and victory follow you, lad!' said the king's daughter.

'I am safe for one night, but the beast will come again and again, until the other two heads come off it.'

He caught the beast's head, and he drew a knot through it, and he told her to bring it with her there to-morrow. She gave him a gold ring, and went home with the head on her shoulder, and the herd betook himself to the cows.

But she had not gone far when this great general saw her, and he said to her, 'I will kill you if you do not say that 'twas I took the head off the beast.'

'Oh!' says she, ''tis I will say it; who else took the head off the beast but you!'

They reached the king's house, and the head was on the general's shoulder. But here was rejoicing, that she should come home alive and whole, and this great captain with the beast's head full of blood in his hand. On the morrow they went away, and there was no question at all but that this hero would save the king's daughter.

They reached the same place, and they were not long there when the fearful laidly beast stirred in the midst of the loch, and the hero slunk away as he did on yesterday, but it was not long after this when the man of the black horse came, with another dress on. No matter; she knew that it was the very same lad.

'It is I am pleased to see you,' said she. 'I am in hopes you will handle your great sword to-day as you did yesterday. Come up and take breath.'

But they were not long there when they saw the beast steaming in the midst of the loch.

At once he went to meet the beast, but *there* was Cloopersteich and Claperstich, spluttering, splashing, raving, and roaring on the beast! They kept at it thus for a long time, and about the mouth of night he cut another head off the beast. He put it on the knot and gave it to her. She gave him one of her earrings, and he leaped on the black horse, and he betook himself to the herding. The king's daughter went home with the heads. The general met her, and took the heads from her, and he said to her, that she must tell that it was he who took the head off the beast this time also.

'Who else took the head off the beast but you?' said she. They reached the king's house with the heads. Then there was joy and gladness.

About the same time on the morrow, the two went away. The officer hid himself as he usually did. The king's daughter betook herself to the bank of the loch. The hero of the black horse came, and if roaring and raving were on the beast on the days that were passed, this day it was horrible. But no matter, he took the third head off the beast, and drew it through the knot, and gave it to her. She gave him her other earring, and then she went home with the heads. When they reached the king's house, all were full of smiles, and the general was to marry the king's daughter the next day. The wedding was going on, and every one about the castle longing till the priest should come. But when the priest came, she would marry only the one who could take the heads off the knot without cutting it.

'Who should take the heads off the knot but the man that put the heads on?' said the king.

The general tried them, but he could not loose them; and at last there was no one about the house but had tried to take the heads off the knot, but they could not. The king asked if there

were any one else about the house that would try to take the heads off the knot. They said that the herd had not tried them yet. Word went for the herd; and he was not long throwing them hither and thither.

'But stop a bit, my lad,' said the king's daughter; 'the man that took the heads off the beast, he has my ring and my two earrings.'

The herd put his hand in his pocket, and he threw them on the board.

'Thou art my man,' said the king's daughter. The king was not so pleased when he saw that it was a herd who was to marry his daughter, but he ordered that he should be put in a better dress; but his daughter spoke, and she said that he had a dress as fine as any that ever was in his castle; and thus it happened. The herd put on the giant's golden dress, and they married that same day.

They were now married, and everything went on well. But one day, and it was the namesake of the day when his father had promised him to the sea-maiden, they were sauntering by the side of the loch, and lo and behold! she came and took him away to the loch without leave or asking. The king's daughter was now mournful, tearful, blind-sorrowful for her married man; she was always with her eye on the loch. An old soothsayer met her, and she told how it had befallen her married mate. Then he told her the thing to do to save her mate, and that she did.

She took her harp to the sea-shore, and sat and played; and the sea-maiden came up to listen, for sea-maidens are fonder of music than all other creatures. But when the wife saw the sea-maiden she stopped.

The sea-maiden said, 'Play on!' but the princess said, 'No, not till I see my man again.' So the sea-maiden put up his head out of the loch. Then the princess played again, and stopped till the sea-maiden put him up to the waist. Then the princess played and stopped again, and this time the sea-maiden put him all out of the

loch, and he called on the falcon and became one and flew on shore. But the sea-maiden took the princess, his wife.

Sorrowful was each one that was in the town on this night. Her man was mournful, tearful, wandering down and up about the banks of the loch, by day and night. The old soothsayer met him.

The soothsayer told him that there was no way of killing the sea-maiden but the one way, and this is it — 'In the island that is in the midst of the loch is the white-footed hind of the slenderest legs and the swiftest step, and though she be caught, there will spring a hoodie out of her, and though the hoodie should be caught, there will spring a trout out of her, but there is an egg in the mouth of the trout, and the soul of the sea-maiden is in the egg, and if the egg breaks, she is dead.'

Now, there was no way of getting to this island, for the sea-maiden would sink each boat and raft that would go on the loch. He thought he would try to leap the strait with the black horse, and even so he did. The black horse leaped the strait. He saw the hind, and he let the black dog after her, but when he was on one side of the island, the hind would be on the other side.

'Oh! would the black dog of the carcass of flesh were here!' No sooner spoke he the word than the grateful dog was at his side; and after the hind he went, and they were not long in bringing her to earth. But he no sooner caught her than a hoodie sprang out of her.

'Would that the falcon grey, of sharpest eye and swiftest wing, were here!' No sooner said he this than the falcon was after the hoodie, and she was not long putting her to earth; and as the hoodie fell on the bank of the loch, out of her jumps the trout.

'Oh! that thou wert by me now, oh otter!' No sooner said than the otter was at his side, and out on the loch she leaped, and brings the trout from the midst of the loch; but no sooner was the otter on shore with the trout than the egg came from his mouth. He sprang and he put his foot on it.

'Twas then the sea-maiden appeared, and she said, 'Break not the egg, and you shall get all you ask.'

'Deliver to me my wife!'

In the wink of an eye she was by his side. When he got hold of her hand in both his hands, he let his foot down on the egg, and the sea-maiden died.

(from *Celtic Fairy Tales*)

The
Kerry Mermaid

by MICHAEL O'REILLY

A tinge of gray faintly illuminating the mottled clouds in the eastern sky was heralding the approach of dawn just as Donal More and his men were coming ashore after having been all night to sea. No sooner had those bronzed fishermen landed than they proceeded to store the fish temporarily — their night's catch — in a hut on the beach, and this task completed they secured their boat in a sheltered cove in close proximity to the hut.

Tired, sleepy, and hungry, the natural impulse of those men was to reach home as quickly as possible, and by the easiest and most direct route. Their way lay along the strand for a mile and from the strand to the public road that led to their homes there was a short, narrow, rocky path between a tall cliff, and at high water this path was impassable. The passage was called Aghgar, the alternate way being a difficult path over a steep mountain, and to avoid this circuitous route, many a desperate risk was taken and many a life was sacrificed in crossing the short but dangerous path of Aghgar.

On coming to Aghgar it was yet dark but not too dark for the men to discern that the tide was receding — a condition that made it possible for stalwart men such as they were to cross with comparative safety. They clasped hands, Donal leading as usual, and no sooner had they entered the passage than they saw before them seated on a rock a woman adjusting her tresses. As soon as she beheld them she seemed to get alarmed, and quick as lightning she disappeared into the water. In her great anxiety to get away, she forgot her mantle, and Donal instantly seized it and held it firmly in his grasp.

'That was the mermaid, or sea-nymph, about which we have heard so much,' said Donal, 'but this is the first time I ever laid eyes on her, though I have been to sea early and late.'

Scarcely had he spoken these words and while yet beneath the cliff, the woman returned and demanded her cloak. With this demand Donal refused to comply, and the mermaid threatened that she would send a mighty wave against the cliff that would overwhelm them and sweep them into the depths of the ocean. This threat did not in the least alarm Donal, for he had often heard that a mermaid had no more power than any other woman after having parted with her mysterious mantle. When the men reached the road she was still following them and ceaselessly imploring Donal to return the garment, but her cries and screams and supplications did not in the least weaken his resolve to retain the cloak, and he folded it carefully and secured it inside his overcoat.

The woman's great distress moved the other men to pity — pity, perhaps, not unmingled with fear. Old Donough acted as spokesman and remonstrated with Donal.

'It is not lucky for you, Donal,' said he, 'to keep such a strange thing, and it is not safe and wise for you to bring it into your fine house, and the mermaid, the poor thing, will drop dead if you keep that cloak.'

'Luck, or ill-luck,' said Donal, 'I will not part with the cloak, and as soon as I reach home, I will lock it in the large trunk.'

The men were pained at Donal's strange behaviour, but save an exchange of ominous looks they did not venture any further persuasion.

When the mermaid understood that there was no prospect of obtaining her cherished garment, she regained her composure and followed Donal meekly to his house where she henceforth took up her abode.

Donal was at this time about thirty years of age, and though

there were hundreds of modest, good-looking, amiable young women within the circle of his acquaintance, he was yet a bachelor. For a man of his station in life, he was possessed of considerable wealth, in fact, he was the richest man in the barony. It was not necessary for him to follow fishing as a means of livelihood, but he always accompanied his men, and he was passionately fond of the sea. There was not from Valentia to Cape Clear an abler boatman than Donal; in the severest storm he could always manage to steer his boat to safety, and he was stalwart, clear-headed, and fearless.

As already stated, the mermaid made Donal's home her abode, and there was not any maid as skillful, as deft, or as zealous in the discharge of her duties. She was a beautiful young woman and Donal first became enamoured of her when he saw her seated on that rock beneath the cliffs at early dawn passing her shapely fingers through her bewitching ringlets.

Shortly a great transformation came over Donal's temperament, he was no longer to be seen with his fishermen and he absented himself from most of the social gatherings of the district. He appointed Donough captain of the boat, and although Donough, too, was an able seaman the men did not have the same confidence in him nor did they give him the same unquestioned obedience that they had unreservedly given to Donal.

'What is coming over Donal at all?' queried Diarmuid. 'He cares for us no more. We miss him very much, and it is many a long night he shortened for us with his stories and songs and pleasant words.'

'I am afraid,' replied Donough, 'that we won't see him very often again in this boat. It was a bad day for us all when he met that mermaid or whatever she is. He is so much in love with her that he has no thought for anyone or anything else. There is a rumour that they are to be married next Sunday.'

'This is queer,' said Diarmuid, 'nobody ever heard of anything like it before. I can't understand how a man of Donal's standing can ever stoop to marry a mermaid that he knows nothing about, and that is not akin to any good old family. However, she is such a beautiful creature that it is hard to blame him for falling in love with her. We all know why Donal was so stony-hearted on the morning that he first met her and why he refused to part with the cloak.'

The attachment of Donal to the mermaid was discussed far and near and many ventured to predict that the mermaid would take Donal to Tír-na-nÓg as Niad had taken Ossian a thousand years before.

Donal and the mermaid were married and there was not in all Kerry a more loving couple than they. Nor had he any reasons to regret his choice, for the mermaid was a dutiful wife and an exemplary mother, and time only still more enhanced her in his esteem. She had an aversion to certain drinks and foods, she never tasted broths or roasted meats, and she would not allow fish of any kind to be brought into the house.

They had been married over thirty years and they were blessed with a large grown-up family. The daughters were like the mother, remarkably handsome, and there were not living at that time any women who approached them in beauty, and they had qualities more enduring than beauty which endeared them to their neighbours and acquaintances. Their sons were tall and stalwart and they inherited their father's passion for the sea. They were leaders in every manly exercise, and there were not in all Ireland more skilled and fearless seamen. Sons and daughters were verily a credit to their parents and their happy home was the rendezvous of scholars, seannachies, and musicians.

Everything prospered with this worthy family, and with wealth came a desire for social distinction. To satisfy this desire they purchased a fine residence in the capital city of the province. All arrangements

having been completed, the moving day arrived; and moving was then even a more formidable task than now, for the vans of over two hundred years ago were rather primitive, and the ideal roads of today were then unknown.

It was long past midday when the heavy-laden wagons were ready to proceed to the city. The family were seated in their coaches ready for the journey when the mother alighted from her coach and returned to the house presumably for something she had forgotten, or perhaps to take another look at the interior of a home in which she had lived so long, where she had spent the happy days of youth, where the children were born, and where she had resided until arrived at serene and contented old age.

On passing through one of the now almost empty rooms — empty of everything worth removing — she noticed that a large trunk that contained miscellaneous old articles had fallen to pieces, and the contents were scattered broadcast on the floor.

She stooped and picked up what appeared to be an old, dust-covered, well-worn garment, and no sooner did she grasp it than she laughed so loudly that her laugh was heard all over the village — if Donal had forgotten the magic mantle, not so had the mermaid. In an instant she regained her former youth and beauty, she no longer cared for husband and children, and swifter than the velocity of the March winds she returned joyfully to her beloved Tír-na-nÓg on the blue rim of the western ocean.

(from *The Gael*)

The Captain in the Box

by J.M. SYNGE

There were two farmers in County Clare. One had a son, and the other, a fine rich man, had a daughter.

The young man was wishing to marry the girl, and his father told him to try and get her if he thought well, though a power of gold would be wanting to get the like of her.

'I will try,' said the young man.

He put all his gold into a bag. Then he went over to the other farm, and threw in the gold in front of him.

'Is that all gold?' said the father of the girl.

'All gold,' said O'Conor (the young man's name was O'Conor).

'It will not weigh down my daughter,' said the father.

'We'll see that,' said O'Conor.

Then they put them in the scales, the daughter in one side and the gold in the other. The girl went down against the ground, so O'Conor took his bag and went out on the road.

As he was going along he came to where there was a little man, and he standing with his back against the wall.

'Where are you going with the bag?' said the little man.

'Going home,' said O'Conor.

'Is it gold you might be wanting?' said the man.

'It is surely,' said O'Conor.

'I'll give you what you are wanting,' said the man, 'and we can bargain in this way — you'll pay me back in a year the gold I give you or you'll pay me with five pounds cut off your own flesh.'

That bargain was made between them. The man gave a bag of gold to O'Conor, and he went back with it, and was married to the young woman.

They were rich people, and he built her a grand castle on the cliffs of Clare, with a window that looked out straightly over the wild ocean.

One day when he went up with his wife to look out over the wild ocean, he saw a ship coming in on the rocks, and no sails on her at all. She was wrecked on the rocks, and it was tea that was in her, and fine silk.

O'Conor and his wife went down to look at the wreck, and when the lady O'Conor saw the silk she said she wished a dress of it.

They got the silk from the sailors, and when the Captain came up to get the money for it, O'Conor asked him to come again and take his dinner with them. They had a grand dinner, and they drank after it, and the Captain was tipsy. While they were still drinking a letter came to O'Conor, and it was in the letter that a friend of his was dead, and that he would have to go away on a long journey. As he was getting ready the Captain came to him.

'Are you fond of your wife?' said the Captain.

'I am fond of her,' said O'Conor.

'Will you make me a bet of twenty guineas no man comes near her while you'll be away on the journey?' said the Captain.

'I will bet it,' said O'Conor; and he went away.

There was an old hag who sold small things on the road near the castle, and the lady O'Conor allowed her to sleep up in her room in a big box. The Captain went down on the road to the old hag.

'For how much will you let me sleep one night in your box?' said the Captain.

'For no money at all would I do such a thing,' said the hag.

'For ten guineas?' said the Captain.

'Not for ten guineas,' said the hag.

'For twelve guineas?' said the Captain.

'Not for twelve guineas,' said the hag.

'For fifteen guineas,' said the Captain.

'For fifteen I will do it,' said the hag.

Then she took him up and hid him in the box. When night came the lady O'Conor walked up into her room, and the Captain watched her through a hole that was in the box. He saw her take off her two rings and put them on a kind of board that was over her head like a chimney-piece, and take off her clothes, except her shift, and go up into her bed.

As soon as she was asleep the Captain came out of his box, and he had some means of making a light, for he lit the candle. He went over to the bed where she was sleeping without disturbing her at all, or doing any bad thing, and he took the two rings off the board, and blew out the light, and went down again into the box.

When O'Conor came back the Captain met him, and told him that he had been a night in his wife's room, and gave him the two rings.

O'Conor gave him the twenty guineas of the bet. Then he went up into the castle, and he took his wife up to look out of the window over the wild ocean. While she was looking he pushed her from behind, and she fell down over the cliff into the sea.

An old woman was on the shore, and she saw her falling. She went down then to the surf and pulled her out all wet and in great disorder, and she took the wet clothes off of her, and put on some old rags belonging to herself.

When O'Conor had pushed his wife from the window he went away into the land.

After a while the lady O'Conor went out searching for him,

and when she had gone here and there a long time in the country, she heard that he was reaping in a field with sixty men.

She came to the field and she wanted to go in, but the gate-man would not open the gate for her. Then the owner came by, and she told him her story. He brought her in, and her husband was there, reaping, but he never gave any sign of knowing her. She showed him to the owner, and he made the man come out and go with his wife.

Then the lady O'Conor took him out on the road where there were horses, and they rode away.

When they came to the place where O'Conor had met the little man, he was there on the road before them.

'Have you my gold on you?' said the man.

'I have not,' said O'Conor.

'Then you'll pay me the flesh off your body,' said the man.

They went into a house, and a knife was brought, and a clean white cloth was put on the table, and O'Conor was put upon the cloth.

Then the little man was going to strike the lancet into him, when says lady O'Conor —

'Have you bargained for five pounds of flesh?'

'For five pounds of flesh,' said the man.

'Have you bargained for any drop of his blood?' said lady O'Conor.

'For no blood,' said the man.

'Cut out the flesh,' said lady O'Conor, 'but if you spill one drop of his blood I'll put that through you.' And she put a pistol to his head.

The little man went away and they saw no more of him.

When they got home to their castle they made a great supper, and they invited the Captain and the old hag, and the old woman that had pulled the lady O'Conor out of the sea.

After they had eaten well the lady O'Conor began, and she said they would all tell their stories. Then she told how she had been saved from the sea, and how she had found her husband.

Then the old woman told her story, the way she had found the lady O'Conor wet, and in great disorder, and had brought her in and put on her some old rags of her own.

The lady O'Conor asked the Captain for his story, but he said they would get no story from him. Then she took her pistol out of her pocket, and she put it on the edge of the table, and she said that any one that would not tell his story would get a bullet into him.

Then the Captain told the way he had got into the box, and come over to her bed without touching her at all, and had taken away the rings.

Then the lady O'Conor took the pistol and shot the hag through the body, and they threw her over the cliff into the sea.

(from *The Aran Islands*.)